Depth Perception

**Read all the books in the
TOM SWIFT INVENTORS'
ACADEMY series!**

TOM SWIFT

INVENTORS' ACADEMY

-BOOK 8-
Depth Perception

VICTOR APPLETON

Aladdin
NEW YORK LONDON TORONTO SYDNEY NEW DELHI

ALADDIN

An imprint of Simon & Schuster Children's Publishing Division
1230 Avenue of the Americas, New York, New York 10020
First Aladdin paperback edition March 2022
Copyright © 2022 by Simon & Schuster, Inc.
Text by Victor Appleton
Cover illustration by Kevin Keele
TOM SWIFT, TOM SWIFT INVENTORS' ACADEMY, and related logos are trademarks of Simon & Schuster, Inc.
Also available in an Aladdin hardcover edition.
All rights reserved, including the right of reproduction in whole or in part in any form.
ALADDIN and related logo are registered trademarks of Simon & Schuster, Inc.
For information about special discounts for bulk purchases, please contact Simon & Schuster Special Sales at 1-866-506-1949 or business@simonandschuster.com.
The Simon & Schuster Speakers Bureau can bring authors to your live event.
For more information or to book an event contact the Simon & Schuster Speakers Bureau at 1-866-248-3049 or visit our website at www.simonspeakers.com.
Cover designed by Heather Palisi
Interior designed by Mike Rosamilia
The text of this book was set in Adobe Caslon Pro.
Manufactured in the United States of America 0222 OFF
10 9 8 7 6 5 4 3 2 1
Library of Congress Cataloging-in-Publication Data
Names: Appleton, Victor, author.
Title: Depth perception / Victor Appleton.
Description: First Aladdin hardcover edition. | New York: Aladdin, 2022. | Series: Tom Swift Inventors' Academy; book 8 | Audience: Ages 8 to 12. | Summary: While working on a service project to clean up a local lake, Tom and his friends begin to question the behavior of famous inventor and project sponsor J.J. Jefferson, who seems unusually interested in the students' inventions.
Identifiers: LCCN 2021033504 (print) | LCCN 2021033505 (ebook) | ISBN 9781665910866 (paperback) | ISBN 9781665910873 (hardcover) | ISBN 9781665910880 (ebook)
Subjects: CYAC: Inventors—Fiction. | Inventions—Fiction. | Service learning—Fiction. | Environmental protection—Fiction. | Camping—Fiction. | Science fiction. | LCGFT: Novels. | Science fiction.
Classification: LCC PZ7.A652 De 2022 (print) | LCC PZ7.A652 (ebook) | DDC [Fic]—dc23
LC record available at https://lccn.loc.gov/2021033504

Contents

Depth Perception

1

The Ejection Expectation

"OKAY, HERE WE GO," I SAID. "IN THREE, TWO, one . . ." I pressed the button, and . . . nothing happened. My thumb depressed the remote again, and I definitely felt the connection engage, but that was all.

"What's the deal, Tom?" Noah Newton asked. My best friend's brow furrowed as his eyes darted from me to the device.

I shook my head. "I don't know."

I gave the rest of the students in my class a nervous glance before I traced the cord leading from the remote switch to our invention. The connections were still in place, so that wasn't the issue.

"You mentioned that you installed a fail-safe switch," Mr. Edge said. "Do you think that's the problem?"

"I'll check," I said as I knelt beside our invention and reached up under its housing.

Our engineering teacher had made a valid point. When Noah and I first introduced our newest invention to the class, we explained that the firing mechanism had a special switch that wouldn't work unless it was submerged in water. The engineering classroom at the Swift Academy of Science and Technology may have been cutting edge, but it wasn't underwater, so we'd needed to bypass the switch for our invention to work.

I felt around beneath the housing until my hand landed on the hard foam ball at the end of a short rod. Water would make the ball float and activate the fail-safe switch. Next I shifted my hand until my fingers brushed the small strip of tape Noah and I had used to hold the ball in place, as if it were underwater. That wasn't the problem either.

I stood up and backed away from our invention. "It's not the fail-safe."

My mind raced as I tried to figure out what had gone wrong. My gaze settled on the large yellow box sitting atop the worktable. It was about half a meter long and half as wide, with one open end. Strapped to the table, the box kind of looked like a miniature garage for a large toy car.

Noah and I were trying to demonstrate (in front of the entire engineering class, embarrassingly enough) how our special housing would eject our underwater drone out of its chute and into the foam pads we'd set up on the other side of the classroom. Why would we create something like that? Well, in theory, the housing would be bolted to the underside of our very own submarine!

Now, building a sub might seem like an ambitious project for a school full of twelve- and thirteen-year-olds, but for students at a school like the Swift Academy, not so much. At our school, it was no big deal to see robots roaming the halls, drones flying overhead, or even students coming up with bigger inventions like ours—just ask Jim Mills about his awesome hovercraft.

"Exciting so far, Swift," Jim said, smirking. Laughter rippled through the rest of the class.

I ignored the comment and continued studying the device. Noah seemed just as nervous as I was as he moved in and double-checked the connections I'd just gone over.

By the way, you might have noticed that I share the same name as our school. The academy wasn't named after me and my innovative inventions, which was quite evident given the failure I was experiencing at the moment. No, the school was named for my father, Tom Swift Sr. Using the proceeds from his next-door tech company, Swift Enterprises, he'd founded a school where brilliant young inventors could excel in science and technology.

I'll tell you one thing, though. At the moment, I wasn't feeling so brilliant.

Noah inspected the back of the launcher while I moved toward the front of the device. Reaching into the launch port, I felt past our underwater drone. The drone was essentially a small, oblong submarine with four covered propellers. Its nose had a clear dome that housed its lights and camera. My fingertips finally brushed over the coiled spring and the release mechanism. Everything was where it was supposed to be—at least, it felt that way.

"Do you two want to figure this out later?" Mr. Edge asked.

"No need," Noah replied. "I see the problem." He bent behind the worktable, then stood back up holding the end of an extension cord. "Nonconductive air gap," he announced as he dangled the cord in one hand. That was our inside joke for when we forgot to plug something in.

The class erupted into laughter. Guess it was an outside joke now.

I pulled my hand from the housing and stepped back just in time.

THUNK!

As soon as Noah plugged in the launcher, the drone shot out of the launch port. I fell back onto the floor as the thing shot across the room and bounced harmlessly into the foam pieces we'd set up. Even though it was only forty-five centimeters long, it sure would've stung if it had hit me.

A loud gasp cut through the quiet before our classmates erupted into laughter again.

"Are you all right, Tom?" Mr. Edge asked as he ran over to my side.

"I'm fine," I replied, rising to my feet. Unfortunately, there hadn't been any foam pieces to protect my backside.

"Dude!" Noah said, coming over. "I guess the trigger was still activated. Sorry about that."

I waved away his concern. "At least we know the launcher works."

Mr. Edge turned to face the other students. "This is a perfect example of why safety should always be our number one priority."

BEEEEEP!

The bell sounded, and everyone gathered their backpacks and shuffled toward the door.

"All right, people," Mr. Edge called over the commotion. "For those of you not attending next week's service project, have a great spring break. I expect all kinds of new ideas when you get back."

Since Noah and I were among those going on the service project trip, we would see Mr. Edge next week. My dad's company had organized a volunteer event to help clean up parts of nearby Lake Carlopa. Now, you may wonder why some academy students would choose a service project over, say, going on a family trip to Disney World. Well, for Swift Academy students, it was a chance to come up with all kinds of sweet new eco-inventions to help with the cleanup. As for Noah and me, it was a chance for us to test out our new submarine. How cool was that?

But for now, Noah and I were definitely going to be the last ones out of the classroom, since we still had to break down our launcher so we could carry it out. Noah crawled under the worktable and began unstrapping the housing while I grabbed the drone and rolled up the foam padding.

After most of the students had filed out, Mr. Edge joined us by the worktable. "That drone nearly took your head off, Tom."

I chuckled nervously. "Yeah, I guess so." Truth be told, I hadn't really thought about the incident that way. I'd been so focused on why the launcher wasn't working that when it finally went off, I was so happy that Noah had solved the problem, that I hadn't really dwelled on the fact that I was almost beaned by the thing.

"Today has me rethinking the safety of your submarine project," Mr. Edge continued.

Noah shot to his feet. "You're not shutting us down, are you?"

Our teacher raised both hands. "I'm not suggesting that. But remember what I said about safety being the number one priority? I think that goes double for an ambitious project like this one."

"For sure," Noah agreed confidently. "We have tons of fail-safes and backups for our backups."

I nodded. "It's true."

"All right," Mr. Edge said with a sigh. "But you need to go over those backups as you test it. Maybe even make a predive checklist."

"Of course," I replied.

Noah held up a thumb. "Everything is going to work perfectly."

Until five minutes ago, I'd shared my best friend's confidence 100 percent. Now I wasn't so sure.

2

The Endurance
Assurance

"THERE'S NOTHING TO WORRY ABOUT," NOAH
said reassuringly. "Everything will be just fine."

Unfortunately, my best friend wasn't trying to quiet my doubts about our upcoming submarine test. His comments were directed at our friend Amy.

"That's what I keep telling her," Sam added.

Amy gave a big sigh. "If you say so."

After school, I'd joined Noah on the front steps, where he was sitting with our friends Samantha Watson and Amy Hsu while they waited for their parents to pick them up. Sam and Amy were the other half of the formidable foursome, as my dad liked to call us.

Noah and Sam were in the middle of what they'd been doing all week—reassuring Amy about the upcoming camping trip. Oh yeah, did I mention that we'd be camping at the lake during the service project? That detail had made the trip even more exciting to most of us. Not Amy, though.

"I thought you were going to do some camping research," I told her. "To make yourself feel better."

Amy, who never had a hair out of place and whose clothes had never met a piece of lint, had also never been camping before. Earlier in the week, I'd suggested she attack the problem like any other—with plenty of research.

"Oh, I did," Amy replied. "And I still am." She jutted a thumb at her backpack resting nearby. "I have the last four camping books the school library had."

"You're going to read all four books by Monday?" Noah asked.

Sam raised an eyebrow. "Who are you talking to?"

Noah grinned. "Oh yeah."

Along with her near-perfect internal clock and precision calculator, Amy had a photographic memory

10

superpower. Heck, if she somehow grew the nerve to sing in front of people, she'd probably have perfect pitch too.

"It was a good idea, Tom," Amy continued. "Getting a handle on the theory before any practical experience." She squirmed a bit. "But it kind of made me more nervous. I came across all these things that could go wrong, especially in the novels I read."

Noah threw his hands up. "You weren't supposed to read novels about camping. It wouldn't be a good story if nothing ever went wrong."

I nodded. "He's right, you know."

"What kind of things are you worried about?" Sam asked.

Amy sighed. "Oh . . . I don't know . . . everything."

"What? Like rain, lightning . . . ," Noah listed, counting on his fingers. "Bugs, snakes, coyotes . . ."

Amy's eyes grew wider with every word.

I chuckled. "I don't think that's helping, dude."

Sam shot him a look. "No, it's not."

"What?" Noah asked with a shrug.

"Don't forget bears," said a familiar voice. "I hear Lake Carlopa is crawling with them."

11

We all turned to see Andrew Foger standing over us. The new arrival to our school enjoyed ribbing anyone around him whenever he got a chance. And I would know, since I grew up with him. Andrew and I used to be friends when we were little, then adversaries, and now friends again . . . kinda.

Sam smiled up at him. "I guess that's why you're not going next week, huh?"

"Please." Andrew gave a dismissive wave. "Like I'm going to spend my spring break picking up trash and sleeping on the ground." He grinned. "I'm going to sit in my air-conditioned house, on my comfy couch, and play *Advanze Skwad* all week long."

Noah's eyes lit up. "Oh yeah! That comes out tomorrow." Noah was always up on the release dates of all the best video games. Part of me was surprised he hadn't planned to kick back on his own couch next week playing the new game instead of helping us.

"Come find me in the game when you're done with your little camping trip," Andrew told Noah. "My gamer tag is SniperKing365. But I'll be way leveled up by then."

Sam rolled her eyes as Andrew moved down the

steps. "At least he's not going to be there next week," she whispered to Amy.

"Hey, he's coming around," I said. It was true. Having known Andrew as long as I had, I thought that last encounter was actually pleasant.

"Coming around, all right," Sam said. "He's gone from obnoxious to simply annoying."

Noah shrugged at me with a *she's got a point* expression.

Sam had never really forgiven Andrew for framing her after he had someone sabotage several people's projects months ago. Students from three different schools had come together at a local summer camp to field-test their inventions. Andrew had gone to a different school back then and had wanted Swift Academy to look bad. It turned out that Andrew had made Sam the perfect scapegoat for everyone's vandalized inventions. So, yeah, I can't say that I really blamed her for holding a grudge.

I turned my attention back to Amy, trying to change the subject, or at least get it back to where it was before Andrew came along. "How about, instead of worrying about all the things that can go wrong, maybe concentrate on the things you can look forward to."

"Yeah," Noah agreed. "I can't wait to see the Beach Comber in action."

Sam and Amy had been working on an invention that would pick up wide areas of litter along the lakeshore. They had been inspired by another invention called the Litterbot 2000, a prize-winning invention created by a student at another school, which had been field-tested at the summer camp. Sam and Amy wanted to build something bigger that could theoretically clean up entire beaches.

Amy's hands fidgeted in her lap. "Yeah, I'm worried about that working too."

Sam rolled her eyes. "It'll be fine. We've tested it enough, haven't we?"

"I guess so," Amy replied with a shrug.

"And what about meeting J. J. Jefferson?" Sam asked. "How cool is that going to be?"

A grin stretched across Amy's face. "I probably won't be able to talk to him, but at least I'll get to be near him."

That was probably the part of the trip I was looking forward to most. The service project was being cosponsored by none other than J. J. Jefferson. Don't know who

I'm talking about? Well, he's a rock star for inventors. He's like the Neil deGrasse Tyson or Bill Nye the Science Guy of the engineering world. My father used to work with him, and, from what my dad said, J. J. Jefferson had jumped at the chance to be a part of the event.

"You think he's bringing Great White?" Noah asked.

I cringed. "I hope not."

"What?!" Noah demanded.

"As cool as it would be to see, that thing would put our sub to shame."

Amy shook her head. "What are you two talking about?"

"Let me show you," Noah said as he pulled out his phone. "J. J. Jefferson came up with this sub that looks and moves like a real shark."

Within moments, Sam and Amy were crowded around Noah's phone as the screen displayed a video featuring Great White in action. The sleek boat snaked through the water, its dorsal fin cutting through the surf. Then it dove, disappearing from view, before breaching the surface in a spectacular jump. The rows of shark teeth painted on the hull gleamed in the sun before it splashed back into the water.

"Whoa!" Amy said.

Sam shook her head. "Why haven't I heard of this thing before?"

Noah shrugged. "Guess you're not cool like me."

Sam gave his shoulder a shove before turning her attention back to the video.

But I couldn't watch any more footage. Thinking of our sub trying to compete with that next week made me anxious all over again, but for a whole new set of reasons.

3

The Unexpected Encounter

DING-DONG.

The doorbell rang, and I ran downstairs. "I'll get it," I called.

Friday night meant pizza for dinner! Most nights, my dad cooks dinner, or we have leftovers. Ever since my mother died a few years ago, he's been big on making sure we share a home-cooked meal almost every night. I even pitch in and cook sometimes. I can make anything you want, as long as you want pancakes. My dad's cooking is great—don't get me wrong—but Friday night pizza had become a fun tradition over the last few months.

I hit the foyer and peeked through the peephole, then gasped when I saw who was standing on the other side. It wasn't either of the usual pizza delivery people. No, it was none other than J. J. Jefferson himself. I froze. Sure, I knew I would be seeing him next week, and I knew he and my father had sometimes worked together. Apparently, I'd even met him when I was a little kid, but I don't remember that. Still, I hadn't been expecting to see him on our doorstep.

I don't know how long I stood there, staring through the peephole, but it must've been a while, because Mr. Jefferson reached out and pressed the doorbell again.

Ding-dong.

I jumped. Finally coming out of my stupor, I unlocked the door and pulled it open. The tall thin man standing on my doorstep looked almost as shocked as I was.

"Tom Jr.?" he asked. "Is that you?"

I nodded, still surprised that *the* J. J. Jefferson was standing in front of me.

Mr. Jefferson shifted a small package to his left hand and reached out with his right. My hand was swallowed in his firm grip. "Well, you've certainly grown since the last time I saw you."

"Thank you," I said, and then tried not to cringe at my stupid reply. I guess I still wasn't over the fact that J. J. Jefferson was in my house. Except he wasn't actually in my house. I was so dumbfounded that I hadn't invited him in. I just stood there, grinning and pumping his hand up and down.

"Uh, come in," I finally got out.

The large man shuffled in just as my father came down the stairs. "Jay!" Dad said. "You made it!"

"What? You think I'd miss pizza night?" Mr. Jefferson asked. "No way that's happening."

I was still in a daze. Not only was J. J. Jefferson in our house, but he also knew about pizza night? This entire thing felt surreal.

My father grinned at me as he shook my idol's hand. "What do you think, Tom? Surprised?"

"Uh . . . yeah," I squeaked out.

"You didn't tell him I was coming?"

My father grinned and shook his head.

Jefferson chuckled. "Oh man. I hope I didn't give you a heart attack."

I forced a nervous smile. "I'm fine. Just shocked, I guess."

Wow, I strung six words together that time, I thought. It was a new record.

"Come on back," my dad told Mr. Jefferson as he led the way toward the dining room.

I was about to follow them (and see if I could string *seven* words together) when I was saved by the bell . . . literally.

Ding-dong.

This time, it was actually the pizza.

While we ate, my dad and Mr. Jefferson mostly discussed different upcoming projects—at least, the ones they could talk about. Even though Mr. Jefferson's company was more commercial and didn't have government contracts like Swift Enterprises, it still had a bunch of products in development that he couldn't discuss before they launched.

I didn't feel bad being left out of the conversation, though. Honestly, it gave me time to get used to the idea that I was having dinner with J. J. Jefferson. At first it was kind of weird, like having dinner with Jeff Bezos or Elon Musk. But the longer I listened to the conversation, the more I realized Mr. Jefferson was a regular person like everyone else. He even picked the olives off his slices of pizza the same way I did.

"Speaking of top secret stuff," Mr. Jefferson said as he slid the mystery box across the table toward me, "I brought something for you, Tom."

I wiped my hands with my napkin, then lifted the lid. Inside the box, a segmented foam base held several components. Four propellers were stacked in one compartment, an RC controller was nestled in another, and a thin, X-shaped device took up the center section. It was a brand-new drone.

"Thanks," I said.

"Now, your dad told me that you already have plenty of drones," Jefferson began, "but this is our brand-new Owl-1. Ultralight design, brushless motors. It's our quietest one yet. That's why we named it after an owl."

"Because owls are virtually silent when they flap their wings," I added.

Mr. Jefferson tapped the side of his head. "Smart kid. Takes after his old man."

"Tell Jay about your drone," my dad said, grinning at me. "The one with the microphones."

I shook my head. "It's not that big a deal."

"I'd like to hear about it," Mr. Jefferson said.

I cleared my throat. "Well, my friend Noah and I made this drone with four directional microphones. But since drone motors are so loud, we came up with a program that matched the frequency of the motors and filtered them out in real time."

Mr. Jefferson raised an eyebrow. "I'm impressed."

"It was mostly Noah," I admitted. "He's an amazing programmer."

"Surround yourself with brilliant people and steal all their ideas to make yourself look smarter." Jefferson jutted a thumb at his chest. "That's the secret to my success."

My dad laughed at his friend's joke. "You'll have plenty to pilfer next week, then. I'm always amazed at what the academy students come up with."

My father and I took turns telling stories about some of the cool inventions my classmates had been working on lately. My dad told Mr. Jefferson about Jim Mills and Jason Hammond's spybots. I mentioned Noah's virtual reality program, which reminded Dad of Amy's cool Pop Chop phone app.

Mr. Jefferson whistled. "Sounds like an exciting place, this academy of yours."

My dad chuckled. "They certainly keep Mr. Davenport, the principal, on his toes."

Mr. Jefferson leaned toward me. "Speaking of cool inventions, I hear you have something special planned for next week."

I shot my dad a look. I couldn't believe he'd told J. J. Jefferson about the sub. Scratch that—of course I could believe it. Dad's always been proud of me and often tells people he works with about my inventions. Embarrassingly often. But did he have to tell the guy with the coolest recreational sub design on the market about my plain, boring sub?

I didn't say any of this, of course. Instead, I muttered, "Uh, yeah. Noah and I built our own sub."

"Nice," Jefferson said with a nod.

"Lake Carlopa is the perfect place to test it," my father added. "It used to be an old rock quarry, so it has great visibility. Tom did his open water dive there."

That was true. A year ago, Dad and I went on a vacation that included a day of scuba diving. My dad was certified but I wasn't. After a week of classes, which included plenty of diving in a swimming pool, I needed to have one open water dive before I could become certified. For my class, that happened at Lake Carlopa.

"It was very cool," I added, happy to be off the subject of my submarine. "And since a bunch of dive instructors use the lake, people have been sinking all kinds of cool stuff to explore there. There's an old school bus, a small plane, and even an armored truck."

"I've heard about the armored truck," my dad said, "but I don't think it was put there for divers." He grinned. "Legend has it that bank robbers crashed it into the quarry before it was a lake. The authorities found the truck, but not the money."

"Oh yeah?" Mr. Jefferson asked, intrigued.

My dad shrugged. "That's how the story goes."

I had seen online pics of most of the wrecks, including the armored truck, which rested at the bottom of the lake next to a small rocky island. This was the first time I'd heard the story behind it, though. I wondered if there was any truth to it, or if it was simply an urban legend.

Mr. Jefferson got to his feet. "All right, Tom. No more changing the subject. Let's see this sub of yours."

"Uh, okay," I said, starting to clear the table.

"I'll take care of these," Dad said as he gently took the plate from my hand.

I felt my face warm as I led the way to the garage. Don't get me wrong, I was proud of Noah's and my creation. It just felt weird showing it to J. J. Jefferson, like I was about to play a song I'd written . . . in front of Mozart.

I opened the door and switched on the light. Our garage, which more often than not doubled as a workshop, had both worktables pushed to the side. The center space was dominated by a large yellow vehicle strapped to a modified boat trailer. Its nose was a clear rounded view port. Two more clear domes served as hatches for the pilot and copilot—or, in nautical terms, the captain and first mate.

"Nice," Mr. Jefferson said as he made a beeline for the vehicle. He ran a hand over its smooth surface, peering into the clear domes.

"Thanks," I said, only realizing after that I'd been holding my breath.

Mr. Jefferson moved to the back of the sub and examined the large propeller inside the extended metal housing. "Propulsion and steering?"

"That's right. We'll maintain positive buoyancy, so

we'll use the propeller to push us down, too."

"Good safety measure," Jefferson said. "If you lose power, you'll just float to the surface."

I nodded and felt myself smiling. It was nice talking with someone who had experience building submarines. If I hadn't been so worried about embarrassing myself, I might've thought of that possible perk sooner.

"How deep can you go?" Jefferson asked as he peered into the cockpit.

"We're using a snorkel to pump in air," I explained. "It's seven meters long."

Jefferson nodded. "Almost twenty-three feet. Nice."

"Noah wanted to build a carbon dioxide scrubber, but we didn't have enough time."

A lot of people think that running out of oxygen is the most challenging problem in designing an underwater vehicle, but the bigger issue is breathing in all the carbon dioxide that's naturally expelled. CO_2 scrubbers work great on regular submarines, but to make our deadline, Noah and I had decided to pump in fresh air from the surface using a long hose connected to a floating platform. Our used air would simply bubble away from the top of the sub through a special one-way valve.

Jefferson knelt and examined the sub's underbelly. "No way!" he cried as he patted the housing between the two metal skids—the same housing I'd just reattached before his surprise visit, and the same one Noah and I had demonstrated in engineering class earlier that day. "You installed an underwater drone launcher? How cool is that?"

My chest swelled with pride. I had impressed J. J. Jefferson.

How cool was that?

4

The Expedition
Evaluation

SITTING IN THE COCKPIT, I TENSED AS I WATCHED the water rush toward me. "Slower!" I called out.

"Slower, please," Noah echoed, albeit more politely.

The brake lights flashed on my dad's SUV, and the trailer hauling our sub and me slowed as it rolled down the boat ramp. Instead of splashing into the water like a newly launched cargo ship, our sub eased into the lake. Noah stood at the top of the cement ramp, watching the process with concern.

When the water level inched toward the open hatch,

I held up a fist. "That's good," Noah called out, and my dad hit the brakes again.

Noah and I had checked and rechecked our calculations when we built our submarine. We'd even had Amy and Sam double-check them. By all accounts, our invention should *not* . . . sink like a stone to the bottom of the lake. Like I had explained to Mr. Jefferson, the sub's positive buoyancy should make it float. Unfortunately, up until this moment, Noah and I hadn't been able to field-test our vehicle, and now we were stuck doing it in front of a bunch of people waiting in line to launch their own boats.

I held my breath as I reached out of the cockpit and lifted the quick-release latch on the strap holding the submarine to the trailer. As soon as the strap fell away, I knew our calculations had been correct. I let out a sigh of relief as I felt the sub rise, bobbing away from the trailer.

"Yes!" Noah cheered.

Grinning, I flicked on the power switch and threw the throttle in reverse. I could hear the propeller churning the water behind me.

"I'll see you at the campsite," I told Noah as I backed away from the boat ramp. He waved before climbing into the passenger side of my dad's car.

I breathed easier as I piloted our sub along the lake's shore. I'd left the front hatch open, so I was enjoying the cool breeze as it ruffled my hair. Step one of our field test had officially been a success; the sub hadn't sunk. For step two, we'd add Noah's weight to find out if we were still buoyant. Step three would be us trying to safely submerge the *Advance*.

Yeah, Noah and I had named our submarine the *Advance*. A little corny, I know, and even kind of ambitious. After all, we knew full well that we weren't the first ones to create a homemade submarine, and we weren't expecting to advance science with this invention. But even so, this was our most ambitious creation yet, and Noah and I were certainly advancing our own horizons.

The boat ramp area slowly fell out of sight as I motored along the shore and around a bend. Because the lake was a flooded rock quarry, instead of declining gradually, like at the beach, the rocky ground pretty much fell off straightaway at the water's edge. That meant I could pilot right next to the shore, which worked in my favor since the lake seemed more crowded than usual. I didn't know how our sub would react to being tossed about in the wake of passing speedboats.

As I cruised along, a familiar landmark came into view—a small island that Noah and I had explored during past camping trips. Its surface was several meters higher than the shoreline, so it loomed like a small fortress a few hundred meters off the main shore. The towering landmass was around ninety-one meters wide—about the size of a football field. Trees and shrubs covered its flat top, but its sides were solid rock. In the past, it hadn't been unusual to see people cliff diving from one of its sheer sides.

It wasn't long until I reached the camping area where we'd be staying. Luckily, my father and Mr. Jefferson were able to score three campsites right on the shore— a campsite for the girls, one for the boys, and one for the adults. Each plot was large enough to house several tents, and each had its own floating dock.

As I neared the site, I spotted Noah standing at the end of the dock on the right. That must've been the one for our campsite.

"Well?" he asked as I pulled up.

"So far so good," I replied. "You want to try her out?"

"You know it," Noah said, "but I have to show you something first."

"What?"

Noah shook his head. "I can't explain it. Okay, I *can* explain it, but it'll be better if you just see it for yourself."

"Okay," I said. Noah's mysteriousness was making me nervous.

I climbed onto the dock and closed the hatch. Then we both tied off the *Advance*, and Noah led the way toward the girls' camping area.

As we crossed the grounds, I noticed litter scattered along the shore. My father had mentioned that he'd asked the park rangers to hold off on cleaning up our area for a week, so volunteers would have the chance to test out their inventions. From what I'd seen so far, we'd have our work cut out for us during the trip.

I followed Noah down the narrow trail until it opened out into a large clearing. There, I saw a picture-perfect campsite scene. Six tents had been erected in a circle, and even though they were different styles and shapes, they were laid out with military precision. A small campfire crackled in the middle, its firewood arranged in a perfect tepee style within a rock ring.

I turned and peered through the trees. I could just make out the boys' campsite. From what I could see through the underbrush, only one tent had been erected so far, and I knew for a fact that Noah and I hadn't set ours up yet.

I turned back to the girls' campsite. Honestly, it could've been for a photoshoot for a camping magazine. "Did they get here a day early or something?"

Noah grinned and shook his head. "Nope." He moved toward the closest tent. Sam was kneeling beside it, digging through a small backpack.

"How did everyone set up so quickly?" I asked. "Did you help them?"

Sam rolled her eyes. "Not me." She pointed across the clearing.

Two tents over, Amy knelt beside Simone Mosby, where she was finishing tying a cord around a stake. "This knot is called a taut-line hitch," Amy explained. "It's adjustable, so you can tighten it to keep the tent from sagging, or if you need extra tension for strong winds."

"Cool, thanks," Simone said.

I looked at Sam in disbelief. "So, Amy's an expert camper now?"

"I blame you, Swift," Sam replied. "You're the one who told her to research camping. I think she memorized every set of tent instructions while she was at it."

"And check out her backpack," Noah added, pointing to the enormous pack propped up near Sam's tent. It was stuffed full of gear and probably as tall as Amy!

"My backpack," Sam corrected. "That's the one she asked to borrow. It's also the one I used when my family hiked the Appalachian Trail for two weeks." Then Sam pointed to the smaller backpack beside it. "*That's* the kind of pack I bring for a four-nighter at the lake."

I chuckled as I watched Amy help Maggie Ortiz and Jessica Mercer toss a line over a tree branch. It looked like they were hanging a bag to keep their food away from bears. "At least she isn't anxious about camping anymore."

"You can say that again," Sam agreed.

"Tom, let's get our tent set up," Noah suggested. "Then maybe we can sneak in another test drive."

"Good idea."

We headed toward the short trail that connected the

three campsites. As we grabbed our gear from my dad's car, he spotted us.

"Your maiden voyage looked good," he said as he screwed together two tent pole segments. "Any issues?"

"So far so good," I replied.

He grinned back at us. "Glad to hear it."

Noah and I were about to take the short trail leading to the boys' campsite when he grabbed my arm. "Whoa, is that who I think it is?" Noah's eyes were practically bugging out of his head.

We watched in awe as an enormous RV pulled into the parking area. Something that big could only belong to J. J. Jefferson. Noah had been jealous when I'd told him about having dinner with the icon the night before, especially the part where I showed off our submarine without him. I hadn't planned any of it, of course, but it was still kind of fun giving my friend grief about it.

"Come on," I said, changing course and heading toward the RV. "I'll introduce you."

"Oh yeah, because you two are big buds now."

After the giant vehicle pulled to a stop, we approached the main door. I could see someone moving behind the tinted glass before it finally swung open.

"Mrs. Scott?" Noah asked, sounding disappointed. "This is your RV?"

Our robotics teacher was dressed in overalls with her hair pulled up with a bandanna as usual. "You fellas can sleep on the lumpy ground all you want," she said as she stepped down from the RV, "but I don't camp. I glamp." She extended a finger toward us. "And spread the word: Don't even bother asking for my Wi-Fi password."

"Yes, ma'am," I replied, swallowing hard.

"Did you *see* the big-screen TV she had in there?" Noah whispered as we hauled our gear toward our campsite.

Noah pointed to an open patch beside a partially assembled tent. "How about that spot there?"

"Wait a minute." I stopped short when I saw who was backing out of the slumped shelter—Terry Stephenson. Noah and I had shared a cabin with him during the summer camp field trip. The kid snored louder than an idling school bus.

Noah's eyes went wide. "Good save."

We found a nice level piece of ground on the *opposite* side of the campsite and got to work.

In record time, our tent was up and our backpacks

stashed inside. I think Noah was as anxious to get back to our sub as I was. The rest of the volunteers would start working on their cleanup inventions soon, so we didn't have long to squeeze in another test run.

We ran back to the dock, and Noah opened the front hatch. "My turn to drive?"

"Definitely," I replied as I lifted the rear hatch and untied the line at the stern.

Noah carefully lowered himself inside as I released the line at the bow. I tossed him the rope and grabbed on to the open rear hatch to keep the sub from drifting away from the dock.

"How's the battery level?" I called.

Noah flicked the power switch. "Ninety-five percent."

"Okay, here goes," I said as I swung a leg into the rear hatch. As I slowly climbed in, I hoped that all our calculations had been correct. I caught my breath as the vessel dipped with my added weight. Luckily, as I settled into the rear seat, the sub bobbed back up again.

Noah reached out of the hatch and pointed to a thin horizontal mark on the sub's hull. The line was where we'd estimated the waterline would be once the craft was launched. Just as we'd predicted, the water gently lapped at the thin line. "Perfect," he said with a grin.

"Looking good, guys," came a familiar voice.

Noah and I glanced up at the dock, but there was no one there. The voice was coming from our left—from the water.

J. J. Jefferson paddled alongside us in a long blue kayak. Dry bags were strapped to the bow and stern, as if he was heading out on a long expedition.

"Hiya, Tom," Jefferson said. "And you must be Noah Newton."

"Yes, sir." Noah gave a small wave.

"Tom's told me a lot about you," Jefferson said. "I may have to steal that noise-canceling program for your drone."

Noah grinned and nodded. "You bet."

I could see my friend swell with pride at the thought of the tech giant wanting to steal his idea. I'd learned firsthand just how much J. J. Jefferson could instill confidence in someone with a few choice words. It was nice to see my friend getting the same treatment.

"Are you two field-testing already?" Mr. Jefferson asked.

"We're not submerging yet," Noah quickly replied.

"This is just a shakedown of the basic controls and a buoyancy check."

"Smart," Jefferson replied.

"Cool kayak," I said. "I—we thought you might show up in a big RV or something."

"Not me," Jefferson said with a shake of his head. "I like to get this beauty out whenever possible." He tapped the side of the kayak. "In fact, I took this baby up a highway in Alaska."

"Up a highway?" Noah asked, scratching his head.

Jefferson smiled. "Well, it's only a road in the winter when it's frozen over. In the summer, it's a nice little ocean inlet full of sea lions, orcas, and humpback whales. Remind me later, and I'll show you some pics."

"Great," Noah said.

J. J. Jefferson dipped his paddle into the water and turned toward the third dock. "I'll catch you later," he called as his kayak glided away.

When Mr. Jefferson was several meters out, Noah grinned back at me. "Dude! That was so cool."

I chuckled. "Are you okay to drive?"

Noah rolled his eyes and faced front again. "Where should we go?"

"Think we have enough power to make it around the island and back?"

"Easily." My friend's confidence was off the charts.

I heard the propeller churn in the water behind me as Noah directed our craft toward the island. It was the perfect landmark for our first two-man field test, and crossing the open water was way more exciting than simply hugging the shoreline.

Our sub moved up and down as we left the relatively calm waters of the shore and began crossing the large expanse that stretched between the docks and the island. There wasn't anyone cliff diving today, and even though the island was usually packed with visitors, only a single large boat was anchored off its sheer edge. As we drew closer, I noticed a blue-and-white flag flying from the boat's stern and remembered from my open water dive that the alpha flag meant that the boat was hosting scuba divers.

"Those are new," Noah said, pointing to one of the many buoys bobbing in the waves around the island, each sporting a red flag with a diagonal white stripe.

"We better turn around," I said.

"Why?"

"Those are diver-down flags," I explained. "That means there are scuba divers in the area. Boats are supposed to steer clear of them."

"Aw man," Noah grumbled as he brought the sub about.

It looked as if the island was off-limits for now. So much for our perfect landmark.

5

The Primary Preliminary

"A LITTLE HIGHER, GUYS," SAM INSTRUCTED.

Noah and I grunted as we raised the left extension. I felt the metal vibrate as Sam slid the retaining pin into place.

"Okay," she said.

We carefully lowered the piece of equipment and moved to the other side of the machine, where we repeated the routine while Amy inserted her pin. I stepped back and wiped my brow. Sam and Amy's Beach Comber was officially assembled.

The large invention resembled a riding mower with

two combs fanning out on either side. Of course the center unit didn't have a seat for a driver. Solar panels lined the top, instead. And there was no steering wheel. Operations would be done remotely by either Sam or Amy. Noah and I had helped them build many of the components, and I couldn't wait to see their Beach Comber in action.

The few volunteers with inventions not focused on the environment would be helping everyone else with theirs. I didn't mind. Swift Academy has always been about collaboration. The arrangement also meant there was a chance to test other inventions during the trip—like our submarine—that would be harder to try out back home. Noah and I had originally planned to make it an official eco-invention by adding robotic arms and a mounted collection bin so we could pick up trash that had sunk in the shallow parts of the lake. Unfortunately, we'd run out of time. Now the *Advance* was an elective invention—one that we'd have to wait to test until after the eco-inventions were up and running.

As a few students and teachers gathered around Amy and Sam's invention, J. J. Jefferson leaned over the Beach Comber and rubbed his hands together. "Who's going to tell me how this works?"

Mr. Jefferson had gone around and introduced himself to all of our classmates. (As if they didn't already know who he was.) That had relieved a lot of the general tension of being on a camping trip with a celebrity.

If I was being honest, Amy was still a little starstruck. She seemed even shyer than usual. Her head dropped as she wrung her hands.

"The combs on either side sift through dirt or sand," Sam explained. "The flexible tines move in waves, pushing any debris toward the center." She nodded at Amy.

Amy took out her phone and tapped on the screen. After a few more taps, the machine came to life, slowly inching across the open shoreline. Hypnotic waves rippled toward the center as each tine pitched forward and back, picking up various bits of litter, forcing them toward the center. A crushed soda can, a candy wrapper, and part of a chip bag gracefully danced toward one another, meeting in the middle. They disappeared under the solar panels only to reappear inside the clear bin mounted on the back of the machine.

"Nice," Jefferson said. "They kind of look like the legs on a millipede."

Sam grinned. "That's where we got the idea."

"Nature has some of the best designs," Jefferson replied. "And always steal from the best, that's my motto."

While Noah and I watched Sam and Amy's invention at work, J. J. Jefferson snapped some pics with his phone before moving on to review other students' inventions. Most of the student volunteers had brought something small to test out, like Kent Jackson's floating trash sifter or Deena Bittick's plastic bag collector, which she'd called the Porcupine. Picture a remote-controlled ball covered in thin ten-centimeter spikes—way cool.

One of the two other large inventions was Jessie Steele's sorter. Using a system of magnets, lasers, and some creative programming, her machine ran collected litter up a conveyor belt and separated out the objects that could be recycled. The long rectangular device had different bins on each side and was covered with, and powered by, six small solar panels. From what I had seen in engineering class, its sorting was impressively accurate.

The final big project was a watercraft, like our sub,

but this one was piloted remotely. Tony Garret and Maggie Ortiz had invented a device to collect litter floating along the shoreline. Their craft consisted of two small pontoons, a little shorter than canoes, with a mesh conveyor belt mounted between them. Floating litter would go up the belt, where it would be collected in a large net stretched along the back. A curved fin on either side of the craft would funnel the litter toward the belt. Like many of the other inventions being tested out on this trip, it was powered by solar energy. They'd named it the *Basker* after basking sharks, which swim along collecting plankton in their open mouths.

I gazed longingly at the lake and Tony and Maggie in their life vests, floating on either side of their craft as they assembled it in the water. Even though I was still a bit anxious about giving the *Advance* a proper underwater test run, the inventor in me was ready to try our newest creation.

After the Beach Comber had traveled several meters, Amy tapped on her phone again to make it stop. She jumped at the light applause from the students and teachers who'd stopped to watch. I don't think she'd noticed that she and Sam had drawn a crowd.

"Nice work," Mr. Edge called.

"Thanks," Sam said. Amy nodded and gave a small smile but didn't say anything.

As everyone went back to their own inventions, Noah and I joined Sam and Amy as they inspected the ground their machine had just covered. A few scraps of litter were still embedded in the earth.

"I think we should lower the arms a bit," Amy suggested. "See if that gets some of that dug-in stuff."

Sam nodded. "Good idea."

"You need help with that?" Noah asked.

Sam pulled a wrench out of her back pocket. "No thanks. We added a simple tension spring on either side."

Noah looked at me and smiled. "You thinking what I'm thinking?"

I grinned and nodded. "Oh yeah." It was sub time!

We turned, ready to head to the dock, when we almost ran right into Mrs. Scott. "Do you know what works best when picking up litter?" she asked holding two pairs of work gloves and two empty garbage bags. "Good old-fashioned elbow grease."

Noah shrugged. "What's elbow grease?"

"Moving the old elbows," she answered, holding out

the supplies. "Doing things by hand. Since it looks like the invention testing has the shore and water covered, why don't you two tackle the woods."

"Yes, ma'am," I said as we took the gloves and bags. It looked like our sub would have to wait.

Noah and I headed into the nearby trees and began picking up litter as fast as possible. I think we'd had the same idea: the sooner we filled our bags, the sooner we'd get to test our submarine.

"I don't get it," Noah said as he held up an empty soda can. "If people come out here to enjoy the great outdoors, why do they trash the place?" His nose wrinkled as he poured out the liquid still inside before tossing the can into his bag.

"Beats me," I replied, pulling a faded, brittle ice bag from a tangle of leaves and twigs. "I guess they think someone else will take care of the mess."

Noah shook his head. "Yeah, and today that someone is us."

We kept at clearing the litter, not worrying about sorting as we went. We'd leave our bags for Jessie's sorter. I was sure she'd be glad to have more material to use to test her invention.

A flash of silver caught my eye, and I dug in the leaves to pull it out before flipping it over. HAPPY BIRTHDAY was written across the other side in big bright letters. I held the Mylar up for Noah to see. "I guess someone's balloon got away from them."

"Oh yeah," Noah agreed; then he shook his head. "Can you believe people still do those big balloon releases? I mean, they know those things have to come down somewhere, right? That's just mass littering, if you ask me."

It was hard not to share my friend's disgust as our trash bags got heavier. If all this litter was from only a week of neglect, I'd hate to see what the campgrounds would look like if the park rangers never came through to clean up.

When our bags were almost full, Mrs. Scott arrived to check on our progress. "You fellas want to put a pin in that for a while? Tony and Maggie have been looking for you. I think they could use your help."

She didn't have to ask us twice. We followed her out of the woods, dropping our gloves and bags near the sorter before veering off toward the shore. Tony and Maggie's invention inched along the water's edge as the conveyor belt sifted out floating garbage.

"I wonder what they need help with," I said. "Everything looks fine from here."

Noah glanced over his shoulder to make sure Mrs. Scott was out of earshot. "Dude, anything's better than picking up trash."

Spotting us, Tony waved as he stepped away from the bank. He had a towel draped over his shoulders, and it looked like he was shivering.

"That water's not cold, is it, this early in the spring?" Noah asked with a smirk.

Tony grimaced and held up his phone. "I tried to get some video of the underside of our invention at work." His phone was encased in a clear pouch. "The video quality isn't so good shooting it through my dry bag."

"The underside, you say?" Noah asked with a sly grin. "Like through the view port of a brand-new submarine?"

Tony nodded. "That's what I was thinking."

Noah and I smiled at each other. "I bet we could arrange that," I said before we took off toward the dock.

I was going to shoot my dad a text, but luckily, we passed him on the way. "Get your radio ready," I said without slowing down. "We're going for a test dive."

"Great!" he replied.

When we reached the sub, Noah unclamped the front hatch while I opened the back one, which had just been resting shut since we'd propped a small solar panel on the dock to charge the *Advance* while we were away. Wires trailed from the panel into the rear hatch, where they attached to the onboard battery.

"What's our charge?" I asked as I leaned inside to remove the clamps from the battery.

Noah reached in and held down a toggle switch, and the battery charge appeared on a small screen. "One hundred percent."

"Nice," I said as I carefully removed a round piece of foam from the back seat.

Noah reached into the back hatch once I was clear. He carefully pulled out a thick coil of hose and wire—our submarine's snorkel. While Noah attached one end to the stern of the submarine, I fastened the other to the float. We'd also added an antenna so we could communicate with whoever had the radio on shore, since we couldn't count on cell coverage being great several meters underwater. I pushed the float into the water and carefully fed out the long hose.

Once everything was set, Noah began to climb into the front hatch.

"Hold up," I called. "My turn to drive, remember?"

Noah grinned. "I was afraid you'd remember that," he said as he moved to the stern.

Once he was past, I stepped into the front opening and reached down to unclip the line from where it was attached to the long rail on the side.

"I can cast you off," Mr. Edge said as he walked out onto the dock.

"Thanks," Noah said, settling into the seat behind me.

"Now, you two be careful," our teacher warned.

I met his eye and felt that wave of anxiety wash over me again. I don't know why, but his concern shook my confidence. Maybe Mr. Edge was especially concerned because I was usually the act-first-and-make-a-plan-on-the-fly guy.

But not this time. Sure, this was our most ambitious invention yet, but I was positive Noah and I had all contingencies covered. We had designed the sub to ascend if it lost power. We had a radio and an onboard compass. We even had an emergency air tank inside. We'd gone through everything that could possibly go wrong and come up with a protocol to address it. Even so, Mr. Edge's concern made me worry that maybe we'd forgotten something.

After Noah and I had both settled in, I gave a nervous wave to our teacher before closing my hatch and pulling the lever that made a watertight seal. "Hatch one sealed," I announced.

"Hatch two sealed," Noah called behind me. "Switching on the air pump."

I heard the switch click, followed by a soft whir. After a couple of seconds, I felt a cool breeze as fresh air began pumping into the sub.

Reaching over, I removed the small radio from its mount. A thin insulated wire connected it to the antenna at the end of the sub's long snorkel. "Radio check."

"I hear you loud and clear," my dad's voice squawked from the tiny speaker. "Be careful and good luck."

"Thanks," I replied before returning the radio to its mount. Then I turned and smiled at Noah through our clear domes. "You ready?"

"Let's do this!"

"Powering up," I announced, reaching for the throttle. Water churned behind us as the sub moved away from the dock.

Turning the small steering wheel, I guided the sub away from shore, bringing us about in a small arc before pushing the wheel away. This motion pulled cables running along the inside of the sub back toward the propeller, angling it down so we'd dive. Water splashed over the front of my dome as the sky disappeared, and the sound of the propeller softened as our submarine slipped completely underwater.

We'd done it. Our submarine worked!

6

The Successful Assessment

"HOW'S IT LOOK, FELLAS?" MY DAD'S VOICE asked over the radio.

Part of me heard his question, but I was too busy gazing at the underwater environment to respond. I smiled as I watched schools of fish swim by. When people walk into a forest, most wildlife scatters and hides. But I'd learned from scuba diving that underwater, the wildlife may flee at first, but they usually come back to investigate.

"Tom," Noah said. "Answer your dad before he thinks we're stuck at the bottom of the lake, or something."

"Oh yeah," I said as I grabbed the radio. "We're good," I told my dad. "Just sightseeing. Sorry."

"Copy that," my father responded. "You two have fun."

I hung up the radio and gripped the wheel with both hands, pushing it forward to make us dive deeper. I glanced over at the onboard depth gauge; we were about two meters below the surface.

"Is this awesome or what?" Noah asked.

"Oh yeah," I replied as I angled us closer to the shore.

As we neared the steep rock face, I turned the wheel, bringing us about so that we were slowly cruising past the wall of rock. If it weren't for the occasional fish swimming by, it would feel as though we were gliding past the side of a mountain.

"*Basker*, dead ahead," Noah announced.

I glanced up and saw Tony and Maggie's invention just above us. It was hard to miss the two pontoons floating parallel to the shore. I turned the wheel, guiding our sub away from the rock face and the *Basker*.

"Where are you going?" Noah asked.

"I'm coming around so our snorkel doesn't snag on their machine."

"Good idea," Noah said as he shifted behind me. "I'll get ready to shoot some video."

I guided the sub a little deeper before coming at the *Basker* from the front. Since the *Advance* has positive buoyancy, hovering in one place would be an issue— our sub would just float to the surface. My plan was to slowly pull forward and then back up, always angling the propeller to push us down each time.

"This is good," Noah said as I brought us closer to the front of the *Basker*.

As I shifted the throttle forward and then in reverse, I glanced up in time to see an old motor oil container float toward the invention's partially submerged conveyor belt. As intended, the green plastic container was caught by the belt and pulled out of the water. Thanks to the holes in the perforated belt, it rode along before dropping into the collection bag in the rear.

"Did you get that?" I asked Noah.

"Oh yeah," he replied. "That was perfect."

Although the machine was sucking up smaller bits of litter, the large bright-green container really illustrated how well the system worked.

"I'm going to get some more footage," Noah said. "Are you good keeping her steady?"

"You bet."

I was surprised how easy it was to keep the *Advance* in one place. Of course, we had gone over several different ways we would theoretically pilot the sub, but neither Noah nor I knew for sure how she would operate until we put our theory into practice. And as long as neither of us got seasick from the slow rocking, hovering in place was a breeze.

After another thirty seconds or so, I heard Noah shuffling behind me. "Tony's going to love this video."

"Let's take this thing a little deeper," I said as I backed the sub away from the *Basker*.

"Ooh, let's check out the scuba divers," Noah suggested. "I bet they won't expect to see something like this."

"You got it." With the aid of our dim red dome light, I checked the compass, then steered us toward the island.

Once we were away from shore, it was as though we were floating inside a green Ping-Pong ball. Even though visibility in Lake Carlopa was better than most places, it wasn't like underwater shots in the movies. We could only see clearly a few meters in every direction, and the deeper we went, the darker things became.

"I'm hitting the lights," Noah announced. With a flick of the switch, our Ping-Pong ball expanded another two meters. A couple of fish darted away as we continued our journey.

I checked the depth gauge. "Four meters down," I announced. "Any leaks?"

There was a pause before Noah replied. "All dry back here."

I glanced around the cramped compartment. I didn't see any leaks either. The deeper we went, the more pressure would build up on the exterior of our sub. We'd calculated for depths well below twenty meters, but it never hurt to check the seams, just to be sure.

"Six meters," I called as the lake bed came into view. Our lights illuminated a blanket of pale silt with the occasional boulder poking through. More fish darted around strands of waving vegetation.

"This is *way* cooler than I expected," Noah said. I heard the giddiness in his voice. He had to be grinning from ear to ear.

As we glided over the eerie landscape, a vertical line

came into view—a thin black rope had been tied to a weighted anchor and stretched to the surface.

"Is that one of the diving buoys?" Noah asked.

I craned my neck to see the rope end at a dark shape bobbing on the waves. "I think so."

"Aren't we not supposed to go past them?"

I shrugged. "I think they're just to keep boats away so they don't run over surfacing divers." I turned the wheel, giving the line a wide berth. "I think we're okay down here. They'll definitely see us coming with our lights on."

Not long after we passed the rope, a wall of rock came into view.

"Dude, what's that?" Noah asked.

"I think it's the island."

"No, off to port," Noah replied. "I mean starboard." He grunted with frustration. "Whatever right is."

"That's starboard," I confirmed as I turned my head to see what he was talking about. I spotted what looked like a particularly large boulder resting on the lake bed. But that wasn't quite right. The object was pale like the other rocks around it, but parts of it were dark. I aimed the sub toward the object to get a better look.

As we cruised closer, more detail came into view. The

object was rectangular and had writing across the top with two dark circles on the far side.

"Cool," I said. "That's the armored truck."

The vehicle was on its side with its roof facing us. Even though the writing on its side was upside down, I could make out the faded lettering: BOLDERO SECURITY.

"Can you get us closer?"

I pushed the wheel forward. "Descending to seven meters."

The end of our snorkel was attached to a very thick float, and, according to our calculations, our sub's motor wasn't strong enough to drag the float underwater. That meant that no matter how deep we tried to dive, seven meters was as low as we could go.

As we neared the truck, I felt our sub slow a bit. I checked the depth gauge, and, sure enough, we were almost seven meters deep. The float was working like a charm.

The vehicle appeared to be a couple of meters below us, and, unfortunately, the closer we got, because of the angle, the harder it was to see the truck through my clear hatch on top. I ducked down to get a better look through the front dome.

"I'm going to squeeze by you," Noah said as he crawled by on my left. "I want to get some shots of this."

I moved to the right as he shimmied through. Thankfully, all the controls and gauges were on that side. Even though it was a snug fit, we'd planned this setup so that one of us could go forward and shoot video through the nose view port if need be.

Once in position, Noah held up his phone and began recording. I worked the throttle and the wheel to slowly circle the truck while keeping the front of the sub aimed toward it. The maneuver was a little easier than when we were recording the *Basker* since the snorkel helped to keep us in position.

Our lights washed over the front of the truck, shining through the cracked windshield and into the empty cab. The truck's front end was crumpled as if it had been in a wreck. The undercarriage was covered in a thin layer of silt, and tiny fish darted around rusted components. One of the double doors at the back lay flat on the lake bed while the other remained shut over the opening.

Even though I'd seen photos and videos of the sunken truck online, it was way creepier in person. The *Advance*'s lights only illuminated partway into the cargo area, and if this were a horror movie, this would be about the time a sea creature would burst from its dark hiding place.

"You fellas still alive?" Noah and I jumped as my father's voice squawked through the radio.

"Man," Noah said, shaking his head. "Not after that heart attack."

I caught my breath and fumbled for the radio. "We're good," I replied instead. "Just checking out the armored truck."

My dad laughed. "Bring me back a bag of cash."

Noah went back to filming. "I think any money down here would've disintegrated by now, don't you?"

"Oh yeah," I agreed, remembering a video where divers opened a spare tank inside the truck to fill part of it with air, like a little underwater cave. "Plus, I've seen tons of pictures of divers exploring the truck. Someone would've found something by now."

Noah turned back to me with a devious grin. "Still, it's the perfect place to launch the drone. Maybe get a better look at what's inside there."

"You're right." As my hand instinctively went to the drone's launch button, my eyes fell on the battery level display. "But maybe we should save that for next time. We're down to fifty percent power."

"Aw man." Noah put his phone away and rolled onto his back. "Since I'm already up here, how about I drive back?"

"Sure," I replied. "Just let me set the controls so we don't bob up while no one's at the helm." I pushed the wheel forward and increased the throttle. The sub angled downward, pulling against the float.

It was awkward, shifting positions, and I tried not to kick my best friend in the face, but I finally shimmied to the rear seat. Once I was in position, Noah made his way to the pilot's seat, where he eased back on the throttle and pulled back the wheel. He circled the wreck as he got a feel for the controls.

"This is the best!" he said with a chuckle.

Although I enjoyed piloting our sub, I had to admit it was fun being a passenger, too. It was nice to just sit back and enjoy the view. I dug out my phone and grabbed some shots of fish as they swam through one of our light beams. Even though my phone was encased in my own clear dry bag, the shots still looked pretty good.

"Okay, I'm taking us back." The sub pitched to one side as Noah turned the wheel.

We cruised just above the lake bed for a while before Noah slowly angled us upward. We glided past the line holding one of the warning buoys.

"Hey, we didn't see any scuba divers," I noted.

Noah shrugged. "Maybe they're diving on the other side of the island."

You would think they'd want to explore the sunken truck. I couldn't remember if there were wrecks on the far side. Still, the anchored boat was big enough to support a large class of fledgling scuba divers. It was a little odd we hadn't come across at least a couple.

I quickly forgot about the boat and its divers when I noticed a large fish swimming beside us and held up my camera to capture some footage as it checked us out with one of its large eyes. I let out a long breath as I recorded the fish slowly moving on, swimming out of our sphere of light. My previous uneasiness and anxiety seemed to drift away with it. Our final sub test couldn't have gone smoother, our calculations had been spot-on, and everything had worked out just as planned.

Turns out, I had been all worked up over nothing.

7

The Speculation Recitation

"AND LAST, BUT NOT LEAST, I'D LIKE TO CON-
gratulate . . ." Mr. Jefferson read from the scrap of paper
in his hand, angling it so light from the campfire could
illuminate the writing. "Alicia Wilkes and her Sea
Sponge. I'm told it did wonders soaking up gasoline
over by the boat ramp. I hope to swipe your final calculations before this is all over. We might be on our way to
creating a new way to clean up oil tanker spills."

I joined the other students and teachers in a hearty
round of applause. That evening, everyone had gathered at the girls' campsite (since it was the best orga-

nized, thanks to Amy) for dinner and a rundown of the day's events. J. J. Jefferson had personally congratulated everyone on their inventions. I sat with Noah, Amy, and Sam atop one of the large logs that had been placed near the fire.

Mr. Jefferson rubbed his stomach. "Oh, and thanks to Amy's delicious cobbler, I may never be able to eat again."

Amy had turned out to be a camping genius. Not only had she helped everyone set up camp (in between working on her invention with Sam), but she'd made dessert in the two large Dutch ovens Sam had brought along. Amy had methodically turned the two coal-covered cast-iron pots until her blueberry cobblers were perfectly done. It was like she had been baking this way her entire life.

As everyone clapped and looked over at us, Amy lowered her head, obviously embarrassed by all the attention.

Sam gave her a nudge as she cheered along with everyone else. "You deserve it, Amy. You're a natural camper."

She shrugged. "It's no different than following a formula in chemistry class."

"Okay, I call Ames as my lab partner from now on," Noah chimed in.

"And now I'd like to turn things over to the cosponsor of this outing, Tom Swift Sr." Mr. Jefferson stepped to the side as my father took his place amid a smattering of applause.

"I agree with Jay that so far our first ecology outing has been a roaring success. And to everyone's delight, not a single student was trapped at the bottom of the lake with their air supply running out." Dad nodded toward Noah and me.

Everyone laughed as they glanced in our direction. I chuckled along with them, while Noah stood and took a small bow.

"Now, before we turn in for the night—" My dad paused, holding up his hand as a wave of grumbling rippled through the crowd. "Those of you who have been camping before will know that morning sunlight and cheerful birdsong make it almost impossible to sleep in, so we'd better hit the sack early." A wide grin stretched across his face. "But what would a campout be without a creepy campfire ghost story first?"

I sat up straighter on our log. I hadn't expected this.

My father reached into his pocket and dramatically pulled out . . . a flashlight. He switched it on and angled it so his face was illuminated from below. Everyone laughed as he scanned the crowd with a grim expression. He waited for everyone to fall silent. "I'm sure you've all seen Tom and Noah's footage of the armored truck," he began.

Not only had Tony and Maggie been thrilled with the video we shot of their invention, but everyone else had also been intrigued by Noah's shots of the sunken truck. He'd passed his phone around, replaying the footage so often, we'd had to borrow Sam's solar panel charger to get more juice.

My father raised an eyebrow. "Well, now I want to tell you about the true story of . . . the Boldero Bandit."

Noah and I glanced at each other. I had heard this story before, of course, but Dad's title was a catchy new addition.

"Many, many years ago there was a daring armored truck heist," my dad explained. "The crooks led the police on a harrowing chase through the streets of Shopton. They evaded every roadblock as the police chased them out of town toward an old, abandoned rock quarry—a quarry that was soon scheduled to be flooded."

My dad paused, gazing around at his captivated audience. "No one knows why they did it, but it was near this very spot that the bandits drove the stolen truck off a cliff, soaring through the air, before crashing into the bottom of the quarry. *Boom!*"

Everyone jumped, and a few people chuckled nervously.

My father squinted. "By the time police and rescue crews made it down to the wreck, there was no one left alive. There was also . . . no money. When the first responders threw open the doors, the back of the truck was completely empty."

Murmurs rippled through the group.

My father shrugged. "Some say there was never any money in the first place—that the bandits had somehow made a mistake and had stolen an empty truck. Others insist the last surviving Boldero bandit hid the loot somewhere in the quarry. Either way, the search for the stolen money was eventually called off, and the city flooded the quarry—armored truck and all—turning the pit into the beautiful lake we know today."

Dad pushed the flashlight closer to his face. Even with the light from the campfire, the flashlight cast creepy shadows around his eyes.

"There are those who think the ghost of the last bandit haunts these shores to this very day." He glanced around. "Some people say if you listen very closely in the dead of night, you can hear his ghostly cries." He cocked his head, as if listening. The rest of us sat transfixed. The campsite was silent, except for the crackling of the campfire.

"WHERE'S MY MONEY?!"

Everyone jumped. A few students, including Amy, squeaked with surprise.

The scared chatter turned to nervous laughter as Mr. Jefferson stepped out from the woods. I'd been so caught up in my dad's story that I hadn't seen the tech genius slip behind us, and, glancing at the faces gathered around the fire, I knew I wasn't the only one.

"I'm sorry," Mr. Jefferson said with a laugh. "I couldn't help it."

Mr. Edge joined my dad. "You got me with that one too," he said as he patted his chest. "All right, everyone. Let's break it up for the night. We made a big dent in the cleanup today, but there's still plenty of litter waiting for us tomorrow."

Everyone got to their feet. Some kids folded their

camp chairs and carried them off with them as the crowd slowly dispersed.

"And don't forget," Sam said, pointing at Noah. "You promised to give me a ride in the sub tomorrow."

"You and everyone else," I added. Thanks to Noah's generosity, it looked as if we'd be spending the next day doing underwater taxi duty.

"I told you everyone would want the *Advance* experience once they saw how cool it was," Noah said. "Besides, whoever's giving sub tours isn't on trash detail."

"Good point." Even though I completely supported cleaning up the park, nothing could ever make picking up other people's junk as fun as cruising around in our sub.

Noah and I said our good-nights to Sam and Amy, then fell into the stream of guys heading back to the boys' campsite. Since we didn't have a super camper like Amy on our side, none of the guys had bothered to build a campfire. Needless to say, the area was pretty dark and also a little eerie as people used the glow from their phones on flashlight mode to make their way to their tents.

After Noah and I climbed inside ours, Noah's phone still illuminated the interior. He lay on his stomach and tapped at his screen.

"What are you doing?" I asked.

"I'm getting the locations of the other wrecks in the lake. Maybe there's something else we can check out in the sub."

"You can get online?" People had been complaining all day about the weak cell signal in the area. Talk about roughing it.

"Shhh! Keep it down, man. If everyone finds out the signal is decent over here, they'll be crowding our tent for the rest of the trip."

"All right," I agreed, stretching out on my sleeping bag and glancing over at his screen. "What did you find out?"

"There's a cool scuba diving site that has them all laid out." Noah pulled up a map of the lake and tilted his screen toward me. Around eight tiny triangles were scattered across the blue area.

I pointed to a triangle beside the island. "That's the armored truck, right?"

"Yup." Noah tapped on the arrow and several images of the truck came up. He scrolled through shots from different angles, some with scuba divers posing in front of and inside the wreck. There was even a thumbnail image linking to the video I'd seen where divers filled part of the rear compartment with air.

Noah went back to the map. "Trouble is, most of the wrecks are on the other side of the lake."

I pointed to one of the far markers. "I think that's the school bus."

Noah tapped the arrow, and, sure enough, dozens of images of the sunken bus filled the tiny screen. It seemed that my diving class wasn't the first to come up with the idea of sitting in the seats for a group shot.

"That would be cool to see," Noah said.

I nodded. "It is."

Noah went through the other markers. He brought up pictures of the sunken airplane, an old army jeep, a rusted pickup truck, an aluminum camper with the windows and doors missing, and two run-down sheds, one of which leaned more than the Tower of Pisa. From the looks of their frailty, they must have been in use way back when the lake was still a rock quarry. They might even have stored explosives back in the day. Unfortunately, the Leaning Shack of Carlopa was the only other sunken object within range of our sub's battery.

"I *guess* we could check it out," Noah said half-heartedly. "If it hasn't fallen over by now."

"We still haven't tested the drone," I said. "We could send it through one of the windows."

"I still want to fly it into the back of the armored truck," Noah said with a grin. "Maybe there's a secret compartment someone missed."

"You just saw all those pics of people inside the thing," I shot back. "You don't think someone's thought to look for a secret compartment before?"

Noah shrugged. "You never know."

"First of all, like you said, any cash underwater for that long is bound to have disintegrated by now. And second, who knows if that's even a real armored truck?"

Noah raised an eyebrow.

I shook my head. "I mean . . . I know it's a real armored truck. But what if it was just placed there for scuba divers, like all the other stuff? My dad could've made up that whole story. He didn't even know about the name Boldero until you showed him the footage." I rolled my eyes. "Besides, he was having way too much fun up there in front of everyone tonight."

Noah nodded. "You could be right. But then why is

the truck the only vehicle on its side? And you saw how the front was all banged up."

I opened my mouth to reply but realized I didn't have an answer.

Noah switched off his phone, and the tent went dark. I heard his sleeping bag rustle as he climbed inside. "Either way, I say sending the drone into the truck is more exciting than using it to look in some old shed."

"You're right there," I agreed. "And the truck won't possibly collapse, trapping our drone inside."

"Man, I didn't think of that," Noah said. "Now I definitely vote truck."

I climbed into my own sleeping bag and went over the launching of the drone in my mind, visualizing everything that could possibly go wrong and what we could do to prevent those scenarios. Just as I'd pictured the shed collapsing, I was doing much better anticipating and planning than I ever had before. Maybe I had finally conquered my act-first-think-later instinct. Then again, maybe not. After all, I didn't think about going to the bathroom first before zipping up the tent and bundling up in my sleeping bag.

I sighed and slowly climbed out of my bag. Noah's

breathing had already slowed, so I knew he was asleep. I did my best to get out of the tent as quietly as possible—no easy task when every zipper movement seems as loud as a chain saw in the still of the night.

After managing to climb out without waking my tentmate, I made my way to the camping area's restroom and shower facility. Since the moon was full and there weren't phone screens glowing everywhere, I could see well enough without my own phone's flashlight.

I swung by the lakeshore on my way back. Bright moonlight glinted off the water, making it look as if I were standing in a black-and-white photograph.

Movement caught my eye, and I instinctively brought up my phone. My mind raced back to Andrew Foger's bear comment. I was ready to switch on the light. I don't know if that would have scared off a bear, but hey, it was all I had on me.

My finger froze over the button on the screen when I realized the motion wasn't a bear. Someone was walking around by the docks. I took a couple of steps forward and saw a tall figure leaning over our sub. Several small flashes of light illuminated the *Advance*, as well as the person taking photographs with his phone. It was Mr. Jefferson.

I crept back into the shadows of the tree line as he left our dock and moved toward his own. I watched him untie his kayak, climb aboard, and push off. He unlatched the paddle from the side of the small craft and paddled away from shore. It seemed strange that Mr. Jefferson would grab pics of our sub before going on a recreational paddle in the middle of the night.

It seemed even stranger when I realized he was paddling all the way to the scuba diving boat anchored by the island.

8

The Exertion Aversion

"MAYBE HE KNOWS THE SCUBA PEOPLE," SAM suggested the next day.

"That's what Noah said," I replied. "And I'll tell you what I told him. . . . Of course he knows them. I can't see someone like J. J. Jefferson being the type to sneak out and spy on people. But why take pics of our sub first?"

Sam didn't reply right away. I couldn't read her expression because I was talking to her legs. They were poking out from under the Beach Comber as she made adjustments to the mechanism.

"He's been photographing everyone's stuff," she finally said.

"And talking about stealing our designs," I muttered.

"He was obviously joking."

I sighed. "That's what Noah said too."

Her right hand waved from under the machine. "Hand me a crescent wrench, will you?"

I grabbed the tool from the nearby toolbox and placed its handle into her outstretched palm.

"Look, maybe he was just going for a quiet night paddle," Sam suggested. "Did you actually see him get into the divers' boat?"

I shook my head. "No. It was too dark and too far away."

Sam slid out from under the Beach Comber. She adjusted her glasses and pulled a twig from her hair. A wide grin stretched across her face. "Okay, so maybe not only does he know them, but he's hired them to search for . . . the lost Boldero treasure."

I should've seen this coming. Sam had always been one to latch on to a good urban legend or conspiracy theory. She totally believed Bigfoot exists and that the government keeps aliens hidden away at Area 51. While she was probably the smartest student at the academy, she loved speculating about the impossible, or at least the improbable.

"I hate to break it to you," I said, "but I think my dad made up that story. I'm pretty sure the armored truck is just another wreck for scuba divers to explore."

Sam shrugged but didn't lose the grin. "If you say so. It looked pretty authentic to me."

As promised, Noah had taken Sam out in the sub first thing that morning. They had toured the armored truck, just as we had the day before. After that, I took Tony Garret for a quick dive. We didn't visit the truck, though; he wanted more footage of the *Basker* in action. It was a pretty boring trip for me, to be honest, but like Noah said, it was better than picking up trash. Once Tony and I returned and our solar panel had recharged the sub's batteries, Noah took Terry Stephenson for a trip. He was still out there, which reminded me . . .

I pulled the radio from my belt and keyed the mic. "Just checking in."

"All good," Noah's voice squawked from the tiny speaker a few seconds later. "We're heading back now."

"Copy that." I returned the radio to my belt.

"I have some more adjustments to make," Sam said, kneeling down, ready to crawl back under the Beach Comber. She pointed her wrench at a nearby trash bag.

"Mind taking another load over to Jessie?"

"You bet." As I grabbed the bag, I was surprised by how heavy it was. It appeared that Sam and Amy's machine had been quite efficient.

I hauled the heavy bag over to where Jessie had set up her sorter. Sam wasn't the only one making adjustments. Jessie crouched beside her long machine, slowly turning a screw with an Allen wrench.

I plopped the bag onto the ground with a grunt. "Here's another load for your . . ." I realized that I didn't know what Jessie had named her invention. "What do you call this thing?"

Jessie shrugged and blew away a long strand of black hair that had escaped her ponytail. "I haven't landed on the right name yet. I've just been calling it the sorter." She pointed at the large triangular funnel on one end. "Dump that in the hopper, please."

I opened the bag and grunted again as I lifted the heavy load up to the hopper. Tilting the bag, I emptied the contents, careful not to spill anything. Once the hopper was full, Jessie pushed a button, and her invention came to life.

Now, one of the cool things about Jessie's sorter is

that she used a long piece of transparent plastic for its cover so you could look past the solar panels and see just how the mechanism operated.

First, the litter spread out over a slow-moving conveyor belt. Next, a set of thin metal tines raked over the trash, pulling out any plastic bags and wrappers that couldn't be recycled, depositing them into the first bin. Then two arms outfitted with magnets took turns waving over the debris as it passed by. When they returned to where they'd started, they ran over a thick brush that knocked away anything the magnets picked up, and metal bits rattled into the second bin. The conveyor belt carried the remaining load through a series of laser beams that detected bits of glass or plastic. I heard jets of compressed air fire as they targeted items, sending them into the third and fourth bins. Finally, all that was left were crumpled aluminum cans. The nonferrous metal that hadn't been caught by the magnets tumbled from the end of the conveyor belt and landed in the final bin. The thing worked like a charm. Sure, there were similar devices at recycling plants, but I bet none of them were portable like Jessie's invention.

"That's amazing, Jessie," I said. "You should name this the Super Sorter."

She smiled. "Hey, I like that. Thanks."

While her invention continued sorting, I made my way to the docks before anyone else could find more jobs for me. I was just in time to catch Noah and Terry tying up the sub.

"Thanks, man," Terry said, giving Noah a fist bump. He turned and offered me one too. "Nice sub, Tom."

"Thanks," I replied, returning the bump.

"I got some sick pics of that wrecked truck," he added. "It was just like your dad said."

As Terry walked up the dock, I helped Noah connect the solar panel to the battery. "It's still at seventy-five percent, since we went straight to the truck and back," Noah reported. "It should be good to go again soon."

"Excellent," I replied. "Amy's already called the next ride." I glanced toward the island. "Did you run into any scuba divers this time?"

Noah shook his head. "None at all. You'd think we would've seen at least one with the way they have the whole place blocked off."

Noah and I left our sub to charge and made the rounds to check out everyone else's projects. Overall, the students and adults were ecstatic with the cleanup. In fact, at the rate we were going, we'd have our section of the lakeshore litter-free well before the trip was over.

The only students who didn't seem completely satisfied were Tony and Maggie. The *Basker* wasn't running efficiently enough for them, and they were brainstorming ways to make it better.

By the time Noah and I made it to Sam and Amy's area, we were surprised to see them watching their invention at work from the comfort of a long bench made from different-size branches.

"Working hard, I see," Noah said as we approached.

The bench creaked as Sam leaned against its long backrest. "Pretty cool, huh? Amy made it."

"No way," I said, moving in for a closer look. Thick branches were neatly lashed together to form the frame. Rows of thinner branches had been secured to the frame to form the seat and backrest. I grabbed a corner and gave it a shake. The thing was surprisingly sturdy. "That's so cool."

"Thanks," Amy said as her hands fidgeted in her lap.

"You're quite the pioneer woman," Noah added.

Amy shrugged. "It wasn't very difficult. The design was in a camp craft book I found in the library."

Sam gave Amy a playful nudge. "And here she was worried about camping. She's a natural."

I glanced up and saw Mrs. Scott holding a couple of pairs of gloves and empty trash bags. She glanced around, clearly looking for *volunteers* for trash detail.

"Are you ready for your ride in the sub, Amy?" I asked.

Amy shot to her feet and grinned. "Oh yeah."

"You think it's charged enough?" Noah asked.

I glanced at the approaching teacher, then back to Noah. "It's charged enough," I said as I handed him the radio.

Noah tracked my eyeline. His shoulders slumped when he spotted Mrs. Scott. "Aw, that's cold, man."

I shrugged, and then Amy and I made our escape.

When we got to the docks, I was happy to see that I hadn't been wrong. Our batteries were charged to 90 percent. I knew from experience that we had more than enough power to get to the armored truck and back.

"Where do I sit?" Amy asked.

I pointed to the rear hatch. "Climb in there, unless you want to drive."

Amy shook her head and moved toward the opening. "I'll leave that to you. And you're sure this is safe?"

"Definitely," I replied.

As she climbed in, I attached the snorkel and untied the rear line, then closed Amy's hatch, showing her how to lock it, before climbing into the front. I was releasing the line when J. J. Jefferson strolled out onto the dock.

"I'm hearing great things about your sub." He held up his phone. "Mind if I get some pics later? Inside and out? I'd really like to study your design."

"Uh, sure," I replied. I didn't get it. Did the ones he'd snuck the night before not turn out well enough?

"I'd ask for an actual ride, but"—Mr. Jefferson gestured to his large frame—"I think things would probably be a little cramped."

I chuckled. "Yeah, I think so."

Mr. Jefferson turned his attention to the open water, pointing to a spot away from the island. "Have you checked out that shack yet?"

I shook my head. "Everyone wants to see the truck." I glanced back at Amy. She nodded inside the clear dome.

"Could be cool," Mr. Jefferson said. "And it would keep you far from those scuba divers."

"We haven't run into them yet," I replied, eyeing him suspiciously. "But we'll be careful."

Mr. Jefferson shrugged. "Okay," he said, but his brow was furrowed.

I closed and latched my own dome before motoring away from the dock. I aimed for the island and opened up the throttle, then turned and looked back at my passenger. "Are you ready to dive?"

Amy nodded and gave a half smile. She gripped the side of the hatch with both hands.

"It'll be fine," I reassured her.

Before I could turn back to face forward, I caught a glimpse of Mr. Jefferson on the dock. His hands were on his hips as he watched us motor away.

9

The Concession Confession

"THIS IS AMAZING," AMY SAID AS WE CRUISED three meters below the surface.

I checked the compass and adjusted my heading. Noah and I had made a note of the truck's location in relation to the dock. That way we could save battery power by not running the external lights until we got there. There was still plenty of light from the surface to see the underwater wildlife in our little sphere of visibility, anyway.

"And look at all the fish," Amy said. "They actually come right up to you."

I told Amy about what I'd learned in scuba class about how curious fish were compared to animals on dry land.

"Speaking of wildlife, have you seen any this trip?" I asked. Kevin Ryan had mentioned coming across a raccoon on his way to the restroom the night before.

"No, thank goodness," Amy said.

"Thank goodness? I thought you liked animals."

"I love animals," Amy replied. "But out here . . ."

I shook my head. "You're not still worried about Andrew's bear story, are you?"

Amy sighed. "Bears, snakes, spiders, bugs. You name it."

"Really? It hasn't been that bad, has it? As for bears, everyone strung the food up in trees away from camp just like you showed them."

"Can I tell you a secret, Tom?" She almost whispered the question.

"Sure," I replied.

"I. Hate. Camping." I couldn't see it, but I heard her jaw clenching behind every word.

That hadn't been what I was expecting. "What are you talking about?"

"I hate sleeping on the hard ground. I miss my bed so much. And I miss taking two showers a day. There's no hot water here, and have you *seen* the showers?"

"Yeah, I know what you mean." The campground showers weren't much more than four walls with openings at the top and bottom. I guess those were for airflow, but it also meant an easy flow of spiders and mosquitoes, too. I didn't know of anyone from our group who'd actually used them yet.

"I hardly got any sleep last night," Amy continued. "You can hear everything through the walls of that thin tent. Every rustling animal, every twig snap, the loud crickets. It was horrible."

I always thought the sounds of the forest at night were kind of soothing, but I could see what she meant, especially if I were homesick and wanted to be in my own bed, safe in my own house.

I checked my watch and the compass before pushing the wheel forward, and we dove another meter.

"But you're so good at camping, Amy."

"I'm good at cleaning our cat's litter box too, but it doesn't mean I like doing it."

I couldn't help but laugh at that one. After a moment,

Amy joined in. When our laughter died, Amy sighed. "I've been going through the motions, doing all the things I researched, trying to take my mind off everything."

"Well, you had me fooled. You're a natural."

"Sam thinks so too," Amy said, her voice rising again. "She invited me to go camping with her family some-time. And they *really* go camping. I'm talking digging-a-hole-for-a-bathroom camping."

"Just tell her the truth," I suggested.

"I'm going to have to. This is my first and *last* camping trip."

I checked my readings again and smiled. "Well, if you want to take your mind off camping for a while, how about checking out this?" I slowed the sub and hit the external lights, revealing the armored truck directly in front of us.

Amy gasped. "Wow!"

Slowly I maneuvered the sub around the wreck. Amy didn't grab any pics with her phone. (We had plenty of those already, anyway). Instead, she gazed out her clear dome as I slowly circled the sunken vehicle. Just as before, I ended the tour at the back of the truck. Our lights barely shone through the open door.

And just as before, we were completely alone with the wreck. There wasn't a scuba diver in sight.

"That's so creepy," Amy finally said. "Can you send your drone in there?"

"Nope," I replied.

"Oh, is something wrong with it?"

I shook my head. "It's just that Noah and I agreed that we wouldn't test the drone until we were together."

"Totally get it," she said. "Not that there's any money in there anyway."

"I know, right?" I'm glad I wasn't the only one who hadn't bought into my dad's ghost story.

"If I were the bandit, I would've buried the money somewhere on the island," she added.

I rolled my eyes. I guess I was still the only one.

"Of course, it wouldn't have been an island back then," Amy continued. "Before the lake was filled in, it would've been more like a mesa. The bandit could also have stashed the money in a cave in the side or something, I guess. Have you and Noah searched for underwater caves?"

"Uh, no." Truth be told, I hadn't even thought of that. "We just checked out the truck."

"Oh, okay."

I glanced down to check the power level. "We're down to sixty percent," I said as I turned the wheel and the wreck disappeared from view.

"Is that enough to get us back?" Amy asked.

"Definitely." The compass spun until we were pointed toward the dock. "Just better safe than sorry. Relax and enjoy the ride."

"Uh, Tom?" Amy asked. "Don't tell anyone about what I said, please."

"Don't worry," I assured her. "Your secret is safe with me, pioneer woman."

Amy laughed. "Thanks."

Until Amy had mentioned it, I had forgotten all about what she'd said about camping. Instead, my mind had been turning over her idea about hidden caves on the side of the island. If someone were searching for a bandit's stash, they probably wouldn't mess with the truck itself. But the sides of the island—that would be the perfect exploration job for scuba divers.

After we docked, I disconnected the snorkel and reconnected the solar panel. Amy returned to her work area while I split off, heading for the boys' campsite. Luckily, I was the only one there.

I stood beside Noah's and my tent, dug out my phone, and took it from its dry bag. Just as Noah had said, I was able to get a decent enough signal to get on the Internet.

I ran a search for *Boldero Security* and *robbery*. To my surprise, I found an old news article from the nineties. I was even more shocked when I read past the head-line. Everything my dad said was right there: the police chase through Shopton, the authorities finally finding the truck crashed in the rock quarry, that there were no survivors, and . . . how the truck had been empty.

My mouth fell open as I lowered my phone. The story of the Boldero Bandit was true.

10

The Improvisation
Reversion

"DUDE, WE *SO* HAVE TO CHECK THAT OUT," NOAH
said as he shoved another empty soda can into his trash
bag.

Even as I helped other students with their projects
and took Kevin Ryan on a quick sub trip, the story
about the Boldero Bandit had consumed my thoughts.
I finally got a chance to show Noah the article once we
were back in the woods, stuck on trash duty. I'd told him
Amy's theory about hiding the money in a cave. "I was
thinking that would be the perfect reason to test our
new drone."

Noah nodded and extended a gloved fist. "You read my mind."

I returned the fist bump before bending down and plucking a faded food wrapper, which had been half-buried in some pine needles. "*If* the scuba divers haven't found it first," I added. "That's probably why we never saw them diving. They're not even bothering with the truck."

Noah shook his head. "Man, they could've been swimming right above us the entire time, checking out the island itself."

"I'm guessing they don't have a cool underwater drone that can slip into tight places, though," I said.

"You know it."

After we'd filled the bags with more litter, I mentioned the other thing that had been on my mind all day. "So, what does J. J. Jefferson have to do with all this? He documents everyone's inventions, then sneaks out to see the divers *and* tries to steer Amy and me away from visiting the truck, pushing us to check out that old shed instead. It can't be a coincidence."

Noah gave me a skeptical look. "What? You think J. J. Jefferson, celebrity engineer, not only wants to steal our designs, but he also hired scuba divers to search for lost money?"

"I don't see why he would. The guy is super rich already." I threw my hands up. "Why would he even pay people money to find . . . more money?"

Noah shrugged. "I don't know. Bragging rights? I've seen a few reality shows where crews search for legendary treasure."

I shook my head. "It doesn't make sense."

Noah's eyes went wide. "I know. Maybe he's the great-grandson of one of the original Boldero Bandits, and he wants to clear his ancestor's name somehow."

I laughed. "Dial it down, Scooby-Doo," I said. "We're not talking about a stagecoach robbery. This took place in the nineteen nineties, not the eighteen nineties."

Noah chuckled. "Oh yeah."

I picked up another crumpled can, shook the dirt from it, and dropped it in my bag. "Either way, I say we suspend sub tours tomorrow and check out the island for ourselves."

"Deal," Noah said with a grin. "This is going to be so cool!"

It took a while to finally fill both our trash bags.

Between everyone's inventions and Noah's and my *elbow grease*, our little part of the park was cleaning up nicely. We dropped off the bags for Jessie's Super Sorter just in time for dinner.

Once again, everyone was impressed with Amy's camping skills. She'd lashed together a rig that suspended several pots over the campfire so a bunch of things could cook at once. The delicious aroma of Mr. Edge's camp stew made everyone even hungrier and more eager to dig in by the time we had gathered to eat. Amy and I shared a knowing glance as he bragged about her natural camping abilities.

Afterward, there weren't any big campfire activities like the night before. No one else had any other spooky stories, and there wasn't a lot to recap about the day's events. Everyone seemed exhausted from all their hard work. There was some discussion among my dad, Mr. Jefferson, and the teachers on whether we should move camp since our area was almost completely litter-free, but like the rest of the students, Noah and I didn't wait around to see how it turned out. Instead, we headed back to our tent and got ready for bed.

While Noah scrolled through his phone, taking

advantage of our secret high-reception area, I mentally went through my checklist for the next day's expedition. I thought we should test the drone as well as the drone launcher while the sub was still docked. Maybe we could tether the drone somehow on the first test, just to make sure it didn't end up at the bottom of the lake. After all, we were here to pick up litter, not add more.

I dug out my phone and began jotting down notes. I didn't even bother taking it out of the dry bag, tapping through the plastic before I forgot any of my ideas.

Then I remembered the antenna. I dug through my backpack and pulled out the special antenna Noah had built for the drone. The small device would attach to one of our phones so we could use an app Noah had programmed to control the drone remotely. That way we wouldn't have to carry yet another device. Plus, it was way cooler being able to drive the drone with a phone *and* see what the onboard camera saw on the screen. I smiled as I dropped the antenna inside the dry bag with my phone.

I had to admit that I was very proud of myself. This entire trip, I'd really been turning over a new leaf when it came to planning ahead.

I was going over how many spare batteries we'd

brought along for the drone when I remembered our sub's battery.

I gave Noah a nudge. "Hey, did you disconnect the solar panel after dark?"

He looked up from his phone, brow furrowed. "Uh ... I don't think so."

I shook my head. "Me neither." I got to my knees and unzipped the tent. "I'll do it real quick."

I slipped on my shoes and switched on my phone's flashlight, then padded down the trail toward the lake. Sometimes charging systems will actually drain a battery if you leave them plugged in after the battery is fully charged. I wasn't sure if our solar panel system worked that way, but I didn't want to take any chances. I wanted a nice full charge for our drone test tomorrow.

When I reached the tree line, just like the night before, I spotted movement beside the docks. Someone crouched by J. J. Jefferson's kayak. I switched off my phone, and my eyes adjusted to the moonlight. I was certain that it was Jefferson again.

I turned and made my way back up the trail. When I was far enough away, I switched on my phone's flashlight and sprinted the rest of the way to our camp. Although

I heard muffled voices coming from some of the tents, I didn't see anyone else walking around outside. Easing up to our tent, I unzipped the flap.

"That was quick," Noah said without looking up from his phone.

"He's doing it again," I whispered.

Noah's head snapped up. "Who's doing what again?"

"J. J. Jefferson. He's kayaking out to that boat again."

Noah sat up and switched off his phone. "Really?"

Right then and there, I had an idea that would definitely break my preparedness streak. I grinned. "Let's follow him."

Noah answered me by shuffling out of his sleeping bag and pushing past me to scramble out of the tent. While he put on his shoes, I zipped up the tent behind me.

Now, I knew that going out in the sub at night was not the smartest idea, but to be fair, we'd given so many tours by then that driving the *Advance* was like second nature to both of us. What was actually gnawing at me was that we didn't have a safety backup. I wished we could leave the radio with someone on the shore like we'd done all day. My mind raced for a solution. I wasn't giving up on my streak that easily.

I unzipped the tent again and reached in to grab the radio. Switching it on, I turned it up to full volume before setting it on the picnic table in the middle of our campsite. I didn't think anyone would mess with it, and if we needed to make contact to get help, someone in the campsite *should* hear our transmission. Just like Amy said, tent material is very thin—somebody would definitely hear "Mayday" being shouted from the radio at full volume.

Noah nodded in approval and then followed me up the trail. I didn't want to risk a light this time, so we moved slowly as our eyes adjusted to the darkness. At the tree line, I stopped and pointed at the dock. Mr. Jefferson was just beginning to paddle away from shore.

"There he goes," Noah whispered.

When he was several meters away, we hustled over to our dock and prepared to set sail. Noah untied the front line and climbed into the front hatch while I disconnected the solar panel and attached the snorkel. I didn't bother arguing with him about who drove (I think it was actually my turn), since I didn't want Mr. Jefferson to hear us. Instead, I gently lowered the float into the water, untied the rear line, and climbed into the stern hatch.

Noah reached out and pushed us away from the

dock. The bow slowly swung out, angling toward the island as we closed and latched both hatches. I hit the power switch, and the interior light came on. What was a tiny red dome light, just bright enough to see the controls, now seemed like a floodlight in the dead of night.

"Man, turn it off. If he looks back, he might see us," Noah said.

"Then let's hurry and get underwater."

Noah hit the throttle and pushed the wheel forward. We were thrown back in our seats as we did what I think was our quickest dive so far. The moonlit water briefly splashed over our domes, and then we were surrounded by darkness. The motor vibrated through the hull, and we gently rocked back and forth like always. With the dark void around us, it felt as if we were standing still. I glanced up to see the dim surface slowly passing above just to make sure we were, in fact, still moving.

"Well, this isn't creepy at all," Noah said.

"You watching the time and the compass?" I asked. "Can you get us to the truck like this?"

"After all the trips I made today, I can get us there blindfolded."

I gave a nervous chuckle. "You kinda are."

Noah pushed the wheel forward, taking us deeper. "You have to admit this is pretty cool. It's like we're flying through space."

I watched the rippling surface fade into darkness. "I think we can hit the external lights once we're at the truck," I suggested. "That should be deep enough that no one above us will notice them."

"Good idea."

We cruised in silence for a while with only the soft hums of the motor and air pump in the background.

"Almost there," Noah announced. "So what's the plan once we get to the truck?"

"We . . . uh . . ." Okay, it was official. I was back to making it up as I went along. The trouble was, I hadn't actually made up anything yet. "Uh . . . I don't know."

"You don't know?!" Noah glanced back at me. "What do you mean you don't know?"

My mind raced to put something together. If we surfaced too early, Jefferson might see or hear us. If he made it to the boat, we surfaced, and we opened our hatches, would we be able to overhear any conversations being held up on deck? What if he ended up going to the island, instead? Should we tie off the sub and follow him? Was there even a place to tie off the sub?

"Well?" Noah demanded impatiently.

My jaw tightened. "You can come up with a plan too, you know."

"I thought you had a plan when you said you wanted to follow him," Noah shot back.

I rubbed the back of my neck. "I don't know. . . . I thought something would just . . . come to me."

"Well, if anything's coming, now's the time to share it."

That's how my superpower usually worked. I'd jump in with half a plan, and the rest worked itself out as I went. It happened all the time. Had I been too focused on seeing that character trait as a flaw? Had I worked so hard to break that cycle that I couldn't do it anymore?

Noah was right. If I was going to come up with something, now really was the time. We had to be close to the truck, so we would have to figure something out quick or just turn around and go back.

In fact, the whole timing thing really nagged at me. It was hard to tell in the dark, but we seemed to be going faster than usual. Noah hadn't been calling out depths like we usually did. Was he even paying attention? I felt a bowling ball form in my stomach.

"Dude, I think you should hit the lights now."

"What?"

"Hit the lights!" I shouted.

Noah flicked the switch, and I squinted as a bright sphere instantly encircled our sub. As my eyes adjusted, the first thing I saw was the wrecked armored truck racing past us. The second was a wall of rock looming in front of us.

"Oh man!" Noah shouted as he pulled back on the throttle. The sub began to slow, but it wouldn't be enough in time. We were hurtling toward the side of the island.

BAM!

Our sub careened into the rock wall, jolting to a stop, and I flew forward, banging my forehead against the inside of my dome. I winced, and the world went dark again as my eyes shut from the pain. Easing them open, I rubbed my aching head. Up front, Noah was doing the same thing.

"Are you all right?" I asked.

Noah grunted. "I feel more stupid than anything else. I can't believe I drove into an island."

I slid back into my seat and glanced around the interior. "We'd better check for leaks."

We went over the interior in silence. From what I

could tell on my end, the cabin had remained bone dry. We still had power—both the interior light and exterior lights remained on—and the air pump hummed on without interruption.

"All good up here," Noah announced.

My stomach knotted as I bent down and looked past Noah at the bow's main view port dome. The hit had felt so strong that I half expected to see cracks spider-webbing across it. Even though all three domes were made from shatterproof plastic, we'd built the protective frame so that it wrapped around the nose of the sub. The strong aluminum must've taken most of the hit, and luckily it wasn't even bent.

I let out a long sigh. "Looks like we built this thing tougher than we thought."

"Yeah," Noah agreed, "but who knew we needed seat belts?"

We both laughed. I think it was more out of relief than at Noah's joke.

But I stopped suddenly when I heard a light tapping on the top of my dome. I glanced up, expecting to see one of the scuba divers knocking on the hatch, checking to make sure we were all right. Instead, pebbles were dropping from the darkness above us and bouncing off the clear plastic. They were followed by larger rocks the size of baseballs. The sound of them striking the hull echoed throughout the cabin.

"What was that?" Noah asked.

"You better get us out of here," I replied. "I think you started a small rockslide."

"On it," Noah said as he turned the wheel left and hit the throttle.

Larger rocks banged against the exterior of our sub as we ran parallel to the rock face. I looked up and gasped when a huge rock—almost as big as the sub itself—entered our sphere of light. It bounced off the side of the island before arcing toward us.

"Faster," I ordered, bracing for impact.

Noah rammed the throttle forward, but it was too late. *WHAM!*

The rock slammed into the sub, pitching us hard to one side. The scene whirled past our view ports as we spiraled out of control.

11

The Exigency Contingency

WHEN THE WORLD FINALLY STOPPED SPINNING, I'd been thrown from my seat and was laid out flat. The dome light flickered off and on, and my entire left side was ice cold, soaking wet with water.

"Tom?" Noah was in a similar position up front. "What happened?"

I slowly sat up, rubbing my sore elbow, just one of the places that hurt after being banged around inside the sub like a pinball. "We got hit by a rock."

"A rock?" Noah asked as he sat up. "How big?"

"*Really* big." I looked out of my dome, now more a

window than a skylight, and saw the lake bed stretching out beyond it. A small fish glanced back at me before swimming on its way. This was not good. Our sub was on its left side, resting at the bottom of the lake.

Noah pushed himself up, putting his hand down in the puddle of water, which was rapidly creeping his way. "Oh man. We're leaking! Where's it coming from?"

While Noah scanned the front, I frantically checked the back and immediately found the culprit. Water gushed from a small pipe poking out of the silent pump in the rear of the cabin.

"Found it," I called. "It's coming from the air pump." I reached out and grabbed the small cap tethered to the pump by a plastic cord, pushing it back against the flow as I screwed it onto the pipe. "I stopped it," I announced.

"So it's pumping water instead of air now?" Noah asked, panic rising in his voice.

I shook my head. "The pump's dead. Water was leaking through, but I capped it."

"How is that possible?"

I crawled toward my dome and pushed my head out as far as it would go, craning my neck to look toward the rear of our sub. A chill washed over me. I didn't see the long hose leading to the surface. "The snorkel's gone."

Noah scrambled to peer out of his own dome. "How can that happen?"

"The force from the rock taking us down must've disconnected it." I slid back out of the dome. "That explains why water was coming through the open hole."

"So, there's no more air coming in," Noah said, eyes wide. "We're going to run out of air!"

I took in a deep breath, trying to calm my own rising panic. "We have plenty of air to reach the surface. See if you can drive us out of here."

My friend just stared back at me with a horrified expression.

I pointed to the controls. "You're driving, remember?"

Noah shook his head. "Right." He spun around and reached up for the throttle. It seemed weird from our new angle, as if the controls were mounted on the wall now. He eased the throttle forward and the motor hummed to life. Unfortunately, we didn't move at all.

"Try reverse," I suggested as I crawled into the dome. I knew we were pinned to the ground somehow, since our sub should've risen to the surface by itself. I shifted around the dome, trying to see how we were trapped, but I couldn't spot anything from my vantage point except a cloud of silt being stirred up from the lake bed by our propeller.

Noah moved the lever in the opposite direction. The motor whined as he gave it full power. Just as before, we didn't shift at all.

I pushed out of the dome and stretched out my arms, bracing against the walls as I rocked us back and forth, trying to dislodge us somehow. Noah saw what I was doing and joined me, all the while alternating the throttle in forward and reverse. I didn't feel the sub move in the slightest. It felt as if we were mounted in cement.

"It's no good," I said, chillingly aware that I was now slightly out of breath. With a limited amount of air left, it hadn't been a good idea to exert ourselves like that.

I took a deep breath and tried to clear my mind, pushing back against the rising terror. Just like I'd learned in scuba class, panicking was the worst thing we could do right now.

Unfortunately, Noah hadn't taken that class with me. He snatched the mic from the radio, his hand trembling as he brought it to his mouth. "Hello?! Can anyone hear me! We're trapped in our sub over by the island!" His eyes were wild as he waited for a response.

I shook my head. "Dude, the antenna was part of the snorkel. No one can pick up our frequency from the bottom of the lake."

As if he had to test my theory, he keyed the mic again. "Hello? Come in, anyone! *Please!*"

He was answered with silence.

I held out a steady hand and stared at him with the best calming expression I could muster. "Look, we have to remain chill and conserve the air we have left."

Noah's face was still panic-stricken. "Oh sure. Because we're not gonna die from lack of oxygen. We'll die of carbon dioxide poisoning way before that happens."

I pointed to the small air tank mounted to the right of the driver's seat. "Don't forget we made a plan for this."

Noah's eyes went wide when he spotted the tank. He unclipped it from its mount and cradled it in his arms like a teddy bear, then his hand ran over the tank's short hose and mouthpiece. "But there's only one regulator."

"We'll take turns," I reassured him. "Just like I told you we did in scuba class."

We had talked about this before, of course, when we were building the sub. We couldn't store two emergency tanks, because they would've added too much weight. I couldn't blame Noah for forgetting that fact now, though, given our current situation.

Noah shook the tank. "But how long will this last us?"

"Long enough for us to figure out what to do," I replied, glancing around, trying to think of what else we could try to dislodge ourselves. My mind raced, but I couldn't come up with anything we hadn't tried already. If the rock was strong enough to drive us past seven meters, snapping off our snorkel, as it pinned us to the lake bed, then it looked like the *Advance* had made its last voyage.

I winced. "Or long enough for us to swim out of here."

"What?" Noah asked, hugging the tank tighter.

"I think we have to bail," I admitted. "We're lucky the rock didn't pin us upside down."

"You call *this* lucky?"

"If the sub was upside down, the hatches would be blocked, and bailing wouldn't even be an option," I explained. "We'd be trapped here." I locked eyes with

115

my best friend. "But we're not trapped, okay? So we have to stay as calm as possible."

Noah closed his eyes and let out a long breath. When he opened them again, he gave me a nod. "You're right. Lucky . . . I guess."

"Okay, first, test the air tank," I instructed.

Noah spun open the valve and put the regulator in his mouth. It hissed loudly as he took in a breath. "All good," he reported.

I crawled toward my hatch and put my hand on the latch. "We open them together, swim outside, then stick together all the way up, right?"

"Right." Noah shuffled toward his hatch and grabbed the handle.

"Just swim to the surface," I repeated. "No big deal, right?" I think I was trying to convince myself as much as I was Noah.

I locked eyes with my best friend through the clear domes. "On the count of three. One . . . two . . ." My eyes widened. "Wait!"

Noah flung his hand away from the handle as if it were red hot. "What?!"

I slid back into the main compartment. "This is

very important. You're going to want to hold your breath all the way up, but you can't."

"What do you mean, I can't?"

"I learned this in scuba class," I said as I pointed to the air tank. "We're breathing compressed air, right? Deep underwater, under all that pressure."

"Yeah, so?"

"So as you swim to the surface and there's less pressure, the air in your lungs is going to expand," I explained. "If you hold your breath, the expanding air can pop your lungs like balloons."

"What?!" Noah's eyes bugged out, and I wished I'd chosen different words.

"But it won't," I reassured him. "You'll be fine. All you have to do is blow a little stream of bubbles from your mouth. It doesn't matter how small. The surrounding pressure will push out the right amount of air."

Noah closed his eyes and grimaced. "Okay, little bubbles. Got it." He slid back toward his hatch.

I grabbed the handle once more. "All right. One, two . . . three!"

We flipped open the latches at the same time, and . . . nothing happened. I was preparing to hold on as water gushed in through the opening. Instead, only a small trickle poured from the seam. I reached up and pushed on the dome. It didn't budge. I saw Noah doing the same thing with no more success.

We really were trapped.

12

The Recovery
Discovery

I BEAT A FIST AGAINST THE DOME, THEN GRUNTED as I shoved it with both hands. My gut twisted in a knot as I felt my panic rising again. Panting, I quickly spun around and tried to kick the hatch open with my feet. Nothing worked.

"Did the rock dent the hull?" Noah asked as he copied my foot maneuver. "Are the hatches bent shut somehow? How can they *both* be stuck?"

I didn't reply. Instead, I stopped my attack on the hatch, took a deep breath, let it out slowly, and tried to calm myself again. The solution was there—it had to be.

In my panic, I was missing it somehow.

We may not have foreseen being pinned to the lake bed, but we'd planned for other kinds of emergencies. We had the radio, the positive buoyancy design, the emergency tank of air . . .

Noah crawled to the nose of the sub. "Do you think we can detach the front somehow?"

My mind went back to the air tank. I'm glad I thought to tell Noah about the dangers of breathing compressed air at this depth. It had been the first thing they taught us in scuba class. But there was something else about the pressurized canister that nagged at my brain. Something to do with the pressure.

I clapped my hands together as the information snapped into place.

Scrambling back, I unscrewed the cap from the air pump. Water immediately gushed out of the pipe and splashed inside.

Noah spun around. "What is that? Water?" he asked. "Are we leaking now too?"

"No," I replied. "I mean . . . yes, we are. I uncapped the air pump."

"What are you doing?" Noah demanded. "Is drowning better than carbon dioxide poisoning?"

I pointed to the tank in his hands. "Look, our sub isn't pressurized like that air tank, right?"

Noah screwed up his face and glared at me. "What?"

I raised an eyebrow. "Right?" I pressed.

Noah threw his hands up. "Okay, right. So?"

I gestured toward the domes. "So, if we were pressurized, those hatches would pop open like soda cans."

Noah's brows drew together. "Yeah, so ..." His eyes widened. "So the pressure is actually greater outside the sub!"

I nodded. "That's what's keeping them shut."

"And you letting in water will equalize the pressure differential," Noah continued with a wide grin. "The hatches should open no problem after that."

A matching grin stretched across my face. Mrs. Lee, our physics teacher, would be proud. I just hoped my idea worked so we could tell her about it someday.

The hardest part of my plan was waiting for the sub to fill with water. I wasn't a naturally patient person, and when you add in our dwindling air supply, the tension increased faster than the sub's carbon dioxide level. Plus, the flickering dome light and the temperature of the water wasn't helping.

Noah shivered as the water covered our legs. "Aw man. This is freezing."

"It'll be warmer closer to the surface," I said from my past diving experience. "But down here at the bottom of the lake? Yeah."

After a few more agonizingly slow seconds, the water level crept halfway up the clear domes. Once it covered them completely, they should swing right open. Even though there was probably plenty of breathable air still trapped inside, Noah and I traded the regulator back and forth, just in case. As the water level reached our waists, I had to stop my teeth from chattering so I could get the thing in my mouth.

The water slowly reached our chests, and our sub's air pocket continued to shrink. Noah took another breath from the regulator and glanced toward the hatches. They were almost completely submerged. "Well?" he asked, passing me the mouthpiece.

"Hang on," I said. I took a breath and handed the regulator back before ducking underwater. The cold nearly made me exhale my entire lungful at once. The flickering dome light barely lit the way as I moved toward the hatch, feeling my way along since everything was one big blur underwater. I wished we'd thought to pack goggles.

My hand brushed against the hatch, and I gave it a shove. Relief washed over me as the dome easily swung open. I scrambled back into the sub, poking my head into the air pocket.

"Well?" Noah asked before taking another breath.

I smiled. "It opened just like we thought."

"Good," Noah said with a shiver. "Let's get out of here."

I moved closer to the hatch. "You ready?"

Noah nodded, taking one more breath from the regulator before handing me the tank. "You better take this. You're a better swimmer." He edged closer to his hatch.

"Okay," I said before taking a breath. "On one . . . two . . . Wait!"

Noah stopped mid-dunk. "Now what?"

"Give me a second." I took a breath and dipped underwater again, feeling my way along until I found the driver's seat. I reached past that until my hand landed on the button I was searching for. I hoped that it still worked underwater as I pressed it. A soft *thunk* outside the sub told me it had. I pushed off the side and poked my head back into our shrinking air pocket.

"What were you doing?" Noah asked, wide-eyed.

"I released the drone," I told him. "Maybe we can come back and see how bad our sub is damaged."

Noah rolled his eyes. "Let's get out of here first, please."

I handed him the regulator for another breath, then took it back to do the same. "Okay, for real this time. One, two . . . three!"

We ducked underwater, and I scrambled through the hatch. Mine was already open, so I was able to swim out of the sub first. Through my blurry vision, I saw Noah push out from his hatch. I quickly grabbed at his hand and pressed the regulator into it. Noah put it in his mouth before we both shoved off from the ground.

With the tank in one hand, and Noah tethered to the regulator, I led the way, kicking and reaching up with my free hand. I focused on the rippling surface, determined to get us to safety. Unfortunately, I was so determined that I completely forgot my own safety rule—I was holding my breath! I loosened my lips and exhaled a tiny stream of bubbles, following them up toward the surface.

Not weighed down by the tank, Noah quickly caught up to me. He shoved the regulator into my chest, trying to give me a turn. I kept kicking as I exhaled the rest of my air before taking another pull from the tank. Noah shot past me.

Swimming in frigid water is hard enough, but swimming in frigid water, fully clothed, wearing shoes, and holding a heavy air tank seemed almost impossible. With Noah's blurry form well above me, I took a calculated risk. I dropped the tank and used both hands to swim up as quickly as possible, concentrating on the moonlit waves and blowing a steady stream of bubbles all the way.

Soon I caught up to Noah, who turned and grabbed at me, no doubt looking for the regulator. I didn't slow down, instead snatching the back of his shirt with one hand and kicking even faster. Noah caught on and continued for the surface. It still seemed a million kilometers away.

My lungs ached, and I felt as if I was expelling too much air as we ascended. It took everything I had to keep blowing bubbles, even though it felt as if my lungs were nearly empty. Fear welled up inside me. I wasn't sure we were going to make it.

After what seemed like a lifetime, my head finally

breached the surface. I gasped for air, getting in a quick breath before sinking back below the waves. I kicked harder, doing my best to tread water despite my soaked clothes as I bobbed up again.

I glanced around, panicking when I saw I was alone. Luckily, Noah popped up about a meter away an instant later. I latched on to one of his flailing arms to keep him above the surface.

"That . . . was not . . . fun," he said between gasps.

"Come on," I said, pulling him toward the island. He began swimming on his own, so I let go and concentrated on our destination. We were only three or four meters from the nearest rocky outcropping. In no time, we were both clinging to the edge of a slippery rock as we caught our breath.

We gasped in silence for a moment before I found a foothold and climbed up the rock, feeling as if I weighed five hundred kilograms as I hauled myself out of the water. Now that we were safe, I collapsed on the large rock. Noah slumped down beside me.

Even though I was soaking wet, the warm spring breeze was welcome compared to the frigid temperature at the bottom of the lake. And I don't know about

Noah, but I felt as if I'd just finished an Olympic swim meet. My arms and legs might as well have been spaghetti noodles.

Noah turned to me, exhausted. "Okay, now what do we do?"

I answered by looking up at the long climb ahead of us to reach the top of the island. Noah followed my gaze and sighed. "I was afraid of that." He lay back on the rock and feebly waved. "You go ahead. I'll wait here until morning."

I shuffled to my feet and turned toward the rock face. Stepping onto a narrow ledge, I hoisted myself up, before grabbing on to another ledge and pulling myself higher. After I'd climbed about a meter, I glanced behind me. Noah was following me after all.

The climb to the top wasn't as bad as I'd thought it would be. The jagged rocks weren't laid out like a natural staircase by any means, but the trip was much easier than standard rock climbing. There were enough protruding ledges that it was no worse than climbing a ladder.

Once I reached the top, I crawled onto the grass-covered surface. I didn't care how many ticks or chiggers

I picked up. It felt too good to be on solid ground again. I spun around and helped Noah over the edge. My legs still felt rubbery, so I quickly backed away from edge before I got to my feet.

I reached into my pocket and pulled out my phone, switching it on through the dry bag, and brought up my father's number. I wasn't looking forward to this call. There was no telling how long I was going to be grounded for taking the sub out at night without telling anyone, but there was no way around it. It was either tell my dad now or spend the night on the island and tell him in the morning.

I got a brief stay of execution—the call didn't go through. I glanced at the screen and saw the problem. "I'm not getting a signal. You?"

The full moon lit Noah's embarrassed face as he pulled his dripping phone out of his pocket.

"What happened to your dry bag?" I asked.

Noah shook his head. "Hello? I didn't think we were going to abandon ship." He shoved the waterlogged device back into his pocket. "My dad is going to kill me."

"Same here," I admitted. "But for a broken sub instead of a broken phone."

Noah winced. "Oh yeah. We are in *so* much trouble."

I peered out over the water toward our campsite. The shoreline was dark, so the campfires must've died down. Only a dim light from the restrooms shone through the trees.

"So what do we do now?" Noah asked. "Wait until morning?"

I shrugged. "I guess we stick to the original plan."

"There was a plan?"

"Yeah," I replied. "Seeing if J. J. Jefferson is looking for the lost money, remember?"

Noah shook his head. "Man, I don't even care anymore. But, hey, maybe that boat can take us back so I can put on some dry clothes."

We stepped down into a small depression in the ground as we made our way along the edge of the island. The surface wasn't completely flat, terraces stair-stepping down along the way. When the scuba boat finally came into view, so did the light from a fire. Someone had set up camp a few terraces below us, next to where the boat was anchored. Three small tents encircled the fire while four people sat around it in camp chairs. One of the figures, even sitting, was much larger than the others. It was none other than J. J. Jefferson.

I ducked down, dragging Noah with me. He seemed annoyed but didn't say anything to blow our cover.

"We've been testing everything at night so no one will see," I heard a woman say.

"And we stayed on the other side of the island after you warned us last night," a man added.

"I know," Jefferson said, rubbing his chin. "And I know it's a big hairy deal to clear out for a couple of days, but some of the kids are beginning to suspect something's up."

Noah and I glanced at each other, eyes wide. We were beginning to suspect, all right. And now we knew for sure! J. J. Jefferson did have people searching for the lost money!

"We could just move the boat," another man suggested. "Hide it on the other side of the island."

"We'd still have to keep the buoys up, though," the woman said. "Otherwise, someone might come to the island and get into everything."

I slowly backed away, motioning for Noah to do the same. With a wave of newfound energy, Noah and I jogged back to where we'd originally emerged from our climb.

"Can you believe it?" I asked when I thought we were far enough away to not be heard.

Noah raised both hands. "I gotta hand it to you, Tom. You called it."

"So what do we do now?"

Noah shrugged. "Go back and ask for a ride to camp?"

"What are you talking about? You heard him. Mr. Jefferson's been trying to keep the search a secret from us."

"So?" Noah asked. "It's not like he's doing anything illegal."

"Are you sure?" I asked. Of course, I wasn't sure either.

"What's he going to do if he finds out we know he has a crew out here?" Noah asked. "It's J. J. Jefferson. He's rich and famous. What? He's going to lock us in the boat until they find the money? Now who's Scooby-Doo?"

I opened my mouth to reply, but Noah didn't let up.

"There's no mystery here, man. No one wants to steal our inventions, and so what if they're looking for lost loot?" He threw his hands up in frustration. "I just want to go back, all right? I'm sick of being cold and wet! I just want to get into some dry clothes and forget this ever happened!"

Before I could answer, the ground fell away beneath our feet. Eyes wide, we scrambled to grab onto something, anything.

Instead, we dropped into darkness.

13

The Remote Remedy

SPLASH!

I was submerged in cold water once more. I held my breath until my feet hit something solid, and I pushed off as hard as I could. When I breached the surface, gasping for air, I was in complete darkness, but Noah's ragged breathing and splashing let me know he was floating nearby. As I treaded water, my hands brushed across something hard. I latched on to the nearby rock with one hand before reaching out for Noah with the other, then pulled him to the edge.

"Aw, come on! What now?" Noah demanded, his voice echoing around us.

With my free hand, I dug my phone out of my pocket. Gripping it tightly so I wouldn't drop it into the water, I carefully brought it up the rock. I turned it on and opened my flashlight app.

The tiny light revealed our latest predicament. We were inside a small cavern about four meters wide. Water filled most of it, but a thin rock ledge ran along one side. I angled the light toward the top of the cave, looking for the opening where we had fallen through. Either the light from my phone was too weak or the cavern was too high, or both; I couldn't see anything clearly.

Noah pulled himself out of the water onto the ledge. I set my phone down as he reached out and hauled me up to join him.

"Thanks," I said. "Are you all right?"

Noah rolled his eyes. "I'm soaking wet again, so no. Not really," he said before going back to examining our surroundings.

Now that I was on the ledge, I raised the phone high above my head and was able to just make out a small hole above us. Scanning the surrounding walls, I searched for any way we might climb back out. Unfortunately, the rock was smooth with almost no handholds. I don't think even a skilled rock climber could've scaled it.

Noah must've come to the same conclusion. He cupped his hands around his mouth and looked up at the hole. "Hello?!" he shouted. "Help!"

I winced as his call reverberated around the cavern. "I don't think anyone's going to hear us this deep."

Noah inhaled, ready to try again, but then stopped, dropping his arms to his sides. He sighed. "What are we going to do?"

I aimed my phone toward the other side of the cave. The cavern wasn't just narrow; it was long. The thin ledge stretched around a curve and out of sight.

"There might be another way out," I said as I edged forward. "Come on."

Leading the way, I shuffled along the ledge, toward the curve. The ceiling of the cave dipped lower, and I ducked as I inched along the rock.

My foot hit something and I stopped. When I shined the light down, I saw the weirdest thing: Someone had stacked several sandbags along the ledge as if they were preparing for a flood. I crouched to get a closer look, gasping when I read the faint writing on one of the bags.

"What is it?" Noah asked.

"Uh . . ." was all I could get out.

On each of the bags the words BOLDERO SECURITY were clearly printed. I swept the light to see farther down the ledge. There must've been a dozen of them neatly stacked there.

"Well?" Noah rested a hand on my shoulder, leaning over to get a better look.

"I think it's the money from the truck," I whispered.

"The what?!" Noah pressed down on my shoulder as he leaned in more. "Dude!"

I reached down and tried to pick up the closest bag, but it felt mushy in my hand, as if it would fall apart if I tried to move it, so I immediately let go.

"Well, let's see," Noah said.

"It feels pretty fragile," I said. "I think the bag might disintegrate if we try to open one of them."

"Oh, okay," Noah said, disappointed. "But banks replace damaged bills, right? We're rich, man!"

I shook my head. "I don't think we're allowed to keep it."

He nudged my shoulder. "I bet there's a big reward, though."

I glanced back to see my friend with his widest grin yet. I think the find had made him forget we were still trapped in a water-filled cavern. "We have to get out of here first," I reminded him.

His smile faded. "Oh yeah."

I aimed the light back down the cavern. The ledge shrank to nothing just past the stack of cash as the chamber funneled down to the water level. It looked like another dead end.

"Here," I said as I handed Noah the dry bag with my phone. He held the light steady as I knelt and slipped back into the water. To my surprise, my feet hit the bottom right away. The water only came up to my chest.

"What are you doing?"

I reached up for the phone. "Looking for a way out. The water got in here somehow, right?" I said as I waded toward the other end of the cave.

"Aw man. You're not thinking . . ."

That's all I heard as I took a breath and ducked underwater. Even though my phone lit the way, everything was a blur. Yet I could just make out what looked like a dark tunnel underwater. I felt around as I moved farther toward the opening, but unfortunately the tunnel

137

seemed to shrink as I went. I had no choice but to back out and come up for air.

"Well?" Noah asked.

I waded back to the ledge. "I don't know. I mean, the lake is right there, so it shouldn't be a big deal to crawl out. But the tunnel keeps getting smaller."

"And the other end might be too small to fit through."

I nodded. Something else I learned from scuba class was that exploring underwater caves was one of the most dangerous diving activities. If you weren't careful, you could wedge yourself into a tight space, becoming trapped there until you ran out of air. And seeing as how neither Noah nor I had air tanks, that wouldn't be very long at all.

Noah backed against the wall and slid down into a seated position. "So we're back to being trapped."

I checked my phone. It only had 30 percent of battery life left. "And about to be in the dark." The flashlight app used a lot of power.

"I say we go back to the hole and yell some more," Noah suggested. "They're bound to hear us sometime."

I didn't reply. Instead, I set my phone on the ledge and carefully opened the dry bag. My plan-as-you-go superpower was in full swing, dialed up to eleven, as my dad always said for some reason.

"What are you doing?" Noah asked.

I pulled out the tiny antenna and plugged it into the phone, then put the entire setup back in the bag. "Remember the drone?"

"Yeah, so?"

"So maybe I can connect to it through the tunnel," I explained as I waded back toward the narrow end of the cavern.

I switched off the flashlight app so I could bring up Noah's remote-control app. I heard a splash behind me just as we were thrust into darkness once more.

"You could've warned someone," Noah said as he waded closer.

I felt him looming over my shoulder as I brought up the app. Hitting a button on the screen, I tried to pair up with our nearby drone. The progress wheel spun for a painfully long time as it searched for a connection.

"This is a long shot, you know," Noah said.

I nodded. "If it doesn't work, we use whatever battery we have left to get back to the hole."

I didn't think anyone would hear us from the nearby

campsite, but by morning, my dad would realize we and the sub were missing. I wasn't looking forward to being the target of a huge underwater search, but hopefully they'd think to check the island. It would take a while, but someone was bound to hear us eventually.

The progress wheel continued to spin. Nothing.

I checked the power level. We were already down to 20 percent. Noah's antenna seemed to suck more juice than the flashlight app.

The tiny wheel spun and spun and spun.

"It was a good try," Noah said wearily.

I sighed, preparing to close the app. My finger was over the button just as *Connected* flashed across the screen. I froze.

"You got it!" Noah said, shaking me so hard I almost dropped the dry bag into the water.

I was excited for a moment but then realized something wasn't right. The screen was still black, and only the buttons for controlling the drone were visible. We should've been looking at the view from the drone's underwater camera by now. "I don't get it. What's wrong?"

"How about switching on the lights," Noah said. I could hear the smugness in his voice.

I shook my head. "Oh yeah."

I tapped the button, and we both jumped as a giant eye stared back at us, filling the entire screen. A moment later, the fish backed up, giving us another curious glance before swimming away.

We laughed as I maneuvered the drone off the bottom of the lake. Silt blew up from the propellers, briefly obscuring our view as it rose and slowly spun around. We both gasped as our submarine came into view. The *Advance* lay on its side, pinned to the lake bed by a slab of granite almost as big as the sub itself.

"Oh man," Noah said. "You're right. We were lucky."

I thought about checking out the sub from another angle, but the battery charge wouldn't last much longer. Instead, I piloted the drone over the sub, carefully scanning the side of the island.

"Want me to drive?" Noah asked.

"How well did that work out last time?"

"That's cold, man."

The view of the rock face continued to scroll down the screen. So far, I was seeing mostly solid rock. We passed a couple of dark holes, and I hoped none of them led to the tunnel in front of us. If they did, there was no way we could fit through them.

"Check it out," Noah said as a large cave came into view. It was huge, like the-size-of-the-rock-that-hit-us huge. The drone's tiny light couldn't penetrate the darkness beyond.

"Think that's it?" I asked. "That looks like where your rock came from."

"*My* rock?"

I held my breath as I drove the drone forward. The hole grew large on the screen as it cruised closer. The sides lit up as the drone motored deeper into the tunnel, though the edges grew narrow the farther it went.

"You know, if this is the wrong tunnel, we're definitely going to lose the signal," Noah said.

"Yeah, probably." I piloted the drone farther in. The shaft shrank some more, but there was still plenty of room to maneuver.

"Dude, look!" Noah said.

I studied the screen closer. There was something weird up ahead.

"Not there," Noah said. He splashed the water in front of us. "There!"

I glanced up from the screen to see light filling the

142

tunnel in front of us. Back on the screen, I spotted our torsos as the drone moved closer to us. I laughed as I backed up, giving the drone room to join us in the cavern.

"There's plenty of room through there for us," Noah said, his grin illuminated by the drone's lights. "We can get out of here!"

I checked my phone. "We only have ten percent power left. We better hurry, or we're going to have to do it in the dark."

"Wait. I have an idea," Noah said. "Let me see your phone."

I handed over the dry bag, and Noah tapped at the screen. "I can have the drone lead us out—just go back the way it came."

It was a brilliant idea. See, when Noah created the remote-control app, he'd designed it so the drone could follow preprogrammed directions, just like the flying drones that create light shows by hovering in formation. He'd also set it up so the drone could remember its previous path and backtrack.

Noah pulled the drone out of the water, spun it around, and aimed it at the mouth of the small tunnel. "Once I tell it to go, you can switch back to your

143

flashlight," he explained. "We can follow the drone's light out of the tunnel if we lose power."

"Good. Let's get out of here." Even though I wasn't complaining as much as Noah, I was sick of being cold and wet too.

Noah tapped the screen and handed my phone back to me. The drone's light moved away as it glided back into the tunnel. I switched on my flashlight as Noah moved closer to the opening and took a deep breath. Then he disappeared underwater.

As I gave him a few seconds' lead, I glanced back at the pile of money bags and grinned. *And Noah said there was no mystery here.*

I took a deep breath before following my friend into the tunnel. Even though everything was blurry, I could easily make out the drone's light in the distance. Noah's swimming silhouette followed closely behind it. There wasn't really room to kick (which was good, since I was worried at first about being kicked in the face by my friend) but that didn't matter. The tunnel had plenty of places to grip. I easily pulled myself along, even one-handed.

For a moment, I thought maybe we had miscalculated. The tunnel suddenly seemed longer and tighter than I'd expected. Even though I couldn't see clearly, my imagination made it stretch out for meters with no end in sight. My lungs began to ache, and panic slowly crept in. *Am I going to run out of air before I reach the end?* I couldn't even see Noah or the drone anymore.

Then the tunnel suddenly widened out, and my hand fell on the edge. I cleared the entrance and pushed off the side of the island, rocketing toward the moonlight above, kicking as hard as I could. After what seemed like an eternity, I finally breached the surface, gasping for air.

I glanced back at the island but didn't see Noah anywhere. Treading water, I spun around and let out a big sigh of relief when I finally spotted him, his head and torso poking above the surface, the drone tucked under one arm while the other held on to Mr. Jefferson's kayak.

The man grinned as he dipped his paddle into the water, moving the boat closer to me. "I'd love to hear the story behind this one."

14

The Impression Reassessment

NOAH AND I HELD ON TO EITHER SIDE OF THE
kayak while Mr. Jefferson paddled us over to the diving
boat. Once we were all on board, he handed us big fluffy
towels. We dried off as best we could, but mostly, it was
nice to wrap up in them.

The three people we'd seen at the camp earlier filed
onto the boat.

"Tom, Noah"—Mr. Jefferson pointed to the new
arrivals—"this is Jim, Dana, and Hector. They work
for me."

We greeted them, barely looking up. Even though

the rest of me was cold, my face felt on fire from embarrassment.

Dana's eyes lit up. "Oh, these are the two with the sub. Jay showed us pics of your design. Nice work, guys."

"Everyone's inventions look great," Hector added. "I can't wait to see them in person."

Noah shot me a look, and I shrugged back at him. I guess I had gotten a little carried away worrying about J. J. Jefferson's photography.

Mr. Jefferson sat on a nearby bench. "All right. Let's hear it. What made you two swim all the way out here?"

Noah and I glanced at each other. "Actually, sir, we didn't swim," I said. "At least, not at first."

We took turns telling the group about our submarine trip, how we were trapped, bailed, and then were trapped again in the water-filled cavern. Mr. Jefferson's eyes grew wider with every twist and turn. We ended up relaying every episode of our misadventure except the part about finding the lost money.

Jefferson shook his head. "Why in the world would you come out here at night, alone? You could've been killed."

Noah and I exchanged another look. "You want to

147

tell him?" Noah raised an eyebrow. "It was your big idea."

"Thanks," I said. I let out a long sigh, surveying my audience. "We were trying to figure out what you were up to, kayaking out to the island at night."

Mr. Jefferson scowled, then nodded toward his crew. He pointed at Noah and me. "You see? This is what I was talking about." He shook his head. "Your father warned me, trying to pull off something like this with all you little geniuses nearby wasn't going to work."

My jaw dropped. "My dad knew about this?"

Jefferson laughed. "Knew about it? It was his idea." He sprang to his feet and lifted the lid of the bench he'd been sitting on. "Now, the question is what we're going to do with the two of you." He bent down and rummaged through the storage area.

My stomach tightened. Even though Noah was being sarcastic, had his suggestion been right? Was Jefferson looking for rope so he could tie us up and keep us on the boat?

"Uh, w-we . . . we w-won't tell anyone," Noah stuttered.

I nodded my head. "Yeah, we promise."

I was shivering—though it could have been because I

was soaking wet—when Mr. Jefferson pulled some kind of weapon out of the bench. Actually, my imagination ran a little wild on that one. What he really held was a large floodlight with a pistol grip.

He smiled. "Do either of you even know *what* you're promising not to tell anyone about?" Before we could answer, he nodded toward the others. "Jimbo, do you mind?"

The younger man smiled. "No problem." He climbed down the ladder and hopped onto the nearby island.

Jefferson motioned us toward the railing and pointed over the side. Noah and I shuffled forward, and I spotted Jim jogging toward four dark shapes floating in the water just off the island's shore. Mr. Jefferson switched on the floodlight and washed its bright beam over them, revealing four tarp-covered objects. The tan shrouds looked like they could've been hiding Jet Skis, but really big ones.

When Jim reached the closest object, he lifted its tarp and revealed a sleek vessel with a glass dome. Its nose was decorated with rows of sharp teeth and one devious eye.

I recognized it at once. "Great White."

Jefferson nodded and switched off the light. "I brought four of them for everyone to try out."

"Way cool!" Noah said.

"Why didn't you tell anyone?" I asked.

"Well, not only was it going to be a surprise," he replied, "but I didn't want to distract anyone from their projects."

Noah nodded. "Oh yeah. Those would be very distracting."

Mr. Jefferson shrugged. "Plus, even though I like to joke about stealing people's ideas, I certainly didn't want to steal the thunder from *your* sub."

"You don't have to worry about that now," Noah said sadly.

"Yeah," I agreed. "The *Advance* is now just another attraction for scuba divers."

Jefferson shook his head. "Man, your dad's going to be furious. What did you think I was doing out here that you'd take a risk like that?"

I rubbed the back of my neck. "We thought you were looking for the Boldero Bandit's money."

"The loot from that old armored truck heist?" Dana asked.

Hector laughed. "You didn't tell us we could be look-ing for lost money out here, boss."

Mr. Jefferson gave a dismissive wave. "No treasure hunting on the job. Besides, it's just an urban legend, anyway."

Noah and I exchanged a look and smiled.

"Actually . . ."

15

The Retribution Resolution

"DUDE, I THINK THIS IS A DIRTY DIAPER. *GROSS!*"
Noah scowled as he chucked a grapefruit-size piece of
litter into his garbage bag. It hit the plastic with a disgusting amount of weight to it. "You'd think they could
give us some grabbers or those sticks with points on
them or something."

I pulled a half-buried, plastic six-pack ring out of
the ground. "We didn't even get those before we were
in trouble."

And we were *so* in trouble.

Mr. Jefferson had ferried us back in his large boat

while everyone was still asleep. That gave Noah and me one last night before news of our adventure spread through camp like wildfire the next morning.

First, we got it from Mr. Edge, then from Mrs. Scott. They both gave us whirlwinds of lectures, containing words like "reckless," "irresponsible," "inconsiderate," and "thoughtless." We'd been put on permanent trash duty for the rest of the trip, and our teachers had both vowed to make us give safety presentations when we returned to school.

My dad's lecture was somehow worse. He'd stood by patiently while the teachers scolded us, then expressed his disappointment and told me I'd shown myself to be untrustworthy. That stung most of all.

After that, he'd grounded me for an entire month, and it wasn't just that I couldn't go anywhere but to school and back home for thirty days. No, this was my dad's seldom-used *nuclear option*. I'd be doing his chores as well as my own, and he suddenly had a long list of projects around the house that he'd been putting off, which were now all mine. But the worst part was, with the exception of homework, I wasn't allowed screens of any kind. That meant no TV, no Internet, no video games, no phone, nothing. In fact, my dad said that unless it came from a tree, I couldn't have any entertainment whatsoever.

I tried to look on the bright side. I loved reading, plus I was planning to use that time to come up with some kind of tool or invention to raise the *Advance* from the bottom of the lake. Like I said before, we came to Lake Carlopa to clean up litter, not leave more behind.

The good thing about having my dad on the camping trip was that I already knew what my punishment was. Noah had to wait until he got home to see how bad he'd have it.

"*Ugh!* I think this was someone's *underwear*." Noah held up a pair of not-so-white tighty-whities. "Are they planting disgusting stuff here to punish us more?"

"At least they let us keep our gloves," I said.

"No kidding."

The last round of reprimands had come from Sam and Amy. Our friends chose different words like "asinine," "idiotic," "insane," and "pea-brained," just to name a few of the tamer ones. Once we'd taken our medicine, we did get to tell them all about our adventure. I even showed them the drone footage on my phone after I'd charged it (since it wouldn't be confiscated until I got home).

I found out that Amy had finally come clean to Sam about not wanting to camp anymore. Sam was understanding, as I'd predicted she would be, and since Amy no longer had to be camper extraordinaire, she came up with the idea to combine the caterpillar combs from the Beach Comber with Tony and Maggie's *Basker*. The undulating tines were much more efficient at driving debris toward the *Basker*'s conveyor belt. That's some Swift Academy collaboration right there!

"Check it," Noah said, gesturing toward the lake. "Here they come again."

We crept closer to the tree line and watched as the four Great Whites cruised into view. They had long tails that swished back and forth, propelling them along. And like their namesakes, they also dipped below the surface, before breaching with small jumps. From our vantage point, we could just make out the smiling students inside the clear canopies.

I think the worst part of our punishment was watching everyone have fun in Mr. Jefferson's sleek subs. We had kept his surprise a secret until the big unveiling.

After that, he and his crew took turns bringing everyone out in the cool watercraft, safely cruising around the cordoned-off scuba area. They even let each of the students drive—something we hadn't even done with our sub! Noah and I hadn't bothered asking if we would get a turn. Then again, we'd already had enough underwater adventure to last a lifetime.

Mrs. Scott caught us watching and glared at us, her eyebrow raised. Our smiles faded as we trudged back into the woods to collect more trash.

Noah picked up an old mason jar and poured out the contents. "I don't even want to know what was in this thing," he said before dropping the empty jar into his bag.

The shark boats hadn't been the only aquatic entertainment during the rest of the trip. Mr. Jefferson and my dad had reported our discovery to Boldero Security. People from the company had come out in park rangers' boats, transporting equipment to the island to recover the stolen money—or what was left of it, anyway. After they carefully removed the bags from the cave, we heard that a little more than half of the cash was salvageable. It turned out there was a reward, but my father talked

Noah and me into donating it to the academy's scholar-ship program. In our current situation, we could hardly refuse, especially after Mr. Jefferson offered to match the donation if we agreed.

We continued picking up litter until our bags were full. Like we had done countless times before, we hauled the heavy loads over to Jessie's Super Sorter. As Noah emptied his bag into the hopper, Mr. Jefferson and my dad walked up from the lake.

"How's it going, fellas?" my dad asked.

Noah shook out the rest of his bag and grabbed mine. "Still finding all kinds of nastiness," he said as he poured.

The men chuckled and exchanged a knowing look.

"You know, guys, I feel partly responsible for your current predicament," Mr. Jefferson began. "I mean, if I wasn't so secretive"—he glanced at my dad, embarrassed—"or was better at hiding my surprise, then maybe a couple of curious students wouldn't have felt the need to investigate."

"And since his surprise was my partly my idea . . ." My dad rolled his eyes. "Well, Jay and I were thinking that *maybe* we've been a little too hard on you."

I felt a glimmer of hope. "You mean I'm not grounded?"

My father burst into laughter. "Good one, Tom. Oh, no. You're still very grounded."

My shoulders slumped.

J. J. Jefferson clasped his hands together. "We thought that it was a little too harsh keeping you two from trying out the Great Whites."

Noah and I looked at each other, eyes wide, mouths open.

Jefferson smiled. "In fact, Dana and Hector are ready for you at the—"

That was all I heard. Noah and I had already thrown our gloves to the ground and were running toward the docks before Mr. Jefferson finished, wide grins stretched across our faces. We may have been grounded when we got home, but in that moment, Noah and I had one last underwater adventure in us!

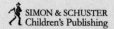

READ& LEARN

with

simon kids

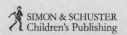

New mystery. New suspense. New danger.

Nancy Drew DIARIES™

BY CAROLYN KEENE

NANCYDREW.COM

EBOOK EDITIONS ALSO AVAILABLE

Aladdin | simonandschuster.com/kids

TWO BROTHERS

MUST RELY ON ALL THEIR

WILDERNESS SKILLS

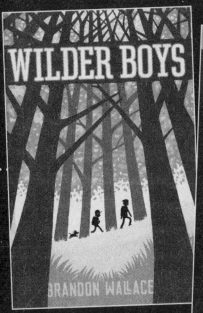

> TO SURVIVE ON THE

ADVENTURE OF A LIFETIME.